P9-DFK-046

"Thoroughly funny
and thrilling."
—*The Washington Post*

"Peck brings more than a
hint of whimsy to his
charming *Secrets at Sea*. A
beguiling humorous tale!"
—*The Christian Science Monitor*

★ "Sheer delight!"—*Kirkus Reviews*

"Delightful!"—*People Magazine*

"Peck, a master at blending
memorable characters, humor,
history, and page-turning
stories, is in top form here."
—*Scripps-Howard News Service*

A *New York Times*
Notable Children's
Book

A *Kirkus Reviews*
Best Children's Book
of the Year

Also by Richard Peck

Secrets at Sea

A NOVEL BY

Richard Peck

ILLUSTRATED BY

Kelly Murphy

PUFFIN BOOKS
An Imprint of Penguin Group (USA) Inc.

PUFFIN BOOKS

Published by the Penguin Group

Penguin Young Readers Group, 345 Hudson Street, New York, New York 10014, U.S.A.

Penguin Group (Canada), 90 Eglinton Avenue East, Suite 700, Toronto, Ontario, Canada M4P 2Y3
(a division of Pearson Penguin Canada Inc.)

Penguin Books Ltd, 80 Strand, London WC2R 0RL, England

Penguin Ireland, 25 St Stephen's Green, Dublin 2, Ireland (a division of Penguin Books Ltd)

Penguin Group (Australia), 250 Camberwell Road, Camberwell, Victoria 3124, Australia
(a division of Pearson Australia Group Pty Ltd)

Penguin Books India Pvt Ltd, 11 Community Centre, Panchsheel Park, New Delhi – 110 017, India

Penguin Group (NZ), 67 Apollo Drive, Rosedale, Auckland 0632, New Zealand
(a division of Pearson New Zealand Ltd.)

Penguin Books (South Africa) (Pty) Ltd, 24 Sturdee Avenue, Rosebank, Johannesburg 2196, South Africa

Penguin Books Ltd, Registered Offices: 80 Strand, London WC2R 0RL, England

First published in the United States of America by Dial Books for Young Readers,
a division of Penguin Young Readers Group, 2011
Published by Puffin Books, a member of Penguin Young Readers Group, 2012

1 3 5 7 9 10 8 6 4 2

Text copyright © Richard Peck, 2011
Illustrations copyright © Kelly Murphy, 2011
All rights reserved

THE LIBRARY OF CONGRESS HAS CATALOGED THE DIAL BOOKS FOR YOUNG READERS EDITION AS FOLLOWS:
Peck, Richard, date.
Secrets at sea / a novel by Richard Peck ; illustrated by Kelly Murphy. p. cm.
Summary: In 1887, the social-climbing Cranstons voyage from New York to London, where they
hope to find a husband for their awkward older daughter, secretly accompanied by Helena and her
mouse siblings, for whom the journey is both terrifying and wondrous as they meet an array of
titled humans despite their best efforts at remaining hidden.
ISBN 978-0-8037-3455-5 (hardcover)
[1. Adventure and adventures—Fiction. 2. Mice—Fiction. 3. Ocean travel—Fiction.
4. Human-animal relationships—Fiction. 5. Social classes—Fiction. 6. Brothers and sisters—Fiction.
7. Atlantic Ocean—History—19th century—Fiction.]
I. Murphy, Kelly, date, ill. II. Title.
PZ7.P338Sdm 2011
[Fic]—dc22 2011001162

Puffin Books ISBN 978-0-14-242183-3

Set in Adobe Jenson
Designed by Jennifer Kelly

Printed in the United States of America

To
Sally Lloyd-Jones

Contents

Secrets at Sea

CHAPTER ONE

Great Change

THE FIRST WE heard of it was when my
sister Louise came skittering down the
long passage from upstairs. Louise skitters.

I forget what Beatrice and I were doing when
Louise flung herself among us. I believe Beatrice
was crumbing the table. We were beginning
to think about lunch, and I'd had some mend-
ing. Our brother, Lamont, would have been at
school. We hoped.

"Louise, pull yourself together," I told her. I
am Helena, the oldest.

Louise had lost her breath and was trying to find it. Her eyes rolled all round the room. She'd tracked in cobwebs on the clean floor. "But wait till you hear—"

"Louise," I said, "did you take the front stairway?"

"Yes," she gasped. "I was in a hurry. Wait till you hear—"

"Louise, we never take the front stairway during daylight. Never. No matter what. We don't do that."

I tried to set a good example for Beatrice. Louise didn't.

"Nobody saw me." Louise heaved. "Nobody ever does." She meant the Upstairs Cranstons. They own the house, but we've been here longer. Generations. "I'm quick and I'm small, and they simply don't see me."

"That younger Cranston girl Upstairs has seen you, Louise," I reminded her. "Camilla Cranston has seen quite a lot of you. Many a time you've crept up to her bedroom in the dead of night. You sit on her bed, and she talks to you. She tells you things. Dead of night, Louise, when everybody is supposed to be asleep. When *you're* supposed to be asleep."

"Yes, well," Louise admitted. "But I haven't come from Camilla's room. And it's not night."

"We know it's not night, Louise," I said, and Beatrice agreed.

"I've been in her mother's room," said Louise. "The one with the cabbage roses in the wallpaper. Mrs. Cranston's room."

Beatrice and I listened.

"They were all in Mrs. Cranston's bedroom, except for Mr. Cranston, of course." Louise made big eyes at us. "They wouldn't have seen me if I'd been sending up flares. They were all talking at the top of their lungs. They were practically running into each other."

"The mother *is* rather loud," I remarked. "And Olive, the older daughter." The family is from somewhere west of here. Cleveland, I believe.

"You couldn't hear yourself think," Louise said. "Even Camilla was aflutter. They were trying on all their hats."

"Hats?" Beatrice piped up. "Why?" She stood there, holding crumbs.

Louise drew herself up importantly. Mother's portrait on the wall looked down upon us. We waited.

"They're going away." Louise's eyes were bigger than her head.

Away? Where? Where did the Upstairs Cranstons ever go? And it was springtime, not summer. In the summer, people went to the mountains and the shore and Saratoga for the races. But not the Cranstons. It took Mrs. Cranston three days to decide to go into Rhinebeck to buy a pair of button gloves.

"Going where?" Beatrice wondered. "You don't mean *moving away*? Packing up and leaving us high and—"

"I'm not sure what I heard, exactly." Louise wavered. "It's something about the girls. About Olive." Louise's mind was in a muddle. "I didn't understand most of it. But Mrs. Cranston went on and on about giving Olive Her Chance. 'We *must* give Olive Her Chance,' said Mrs. Cranston."

The eyes in my mind narrowed. I am Helena, the oldest, and I needed to understand everything. "Where are they going, Louise?"

"Europe," Louise said. Just that one word like the crack of doom.

"Where's that?" Beatrice was agog.

Louise said, "Europe is across the—"

"Never mind where it is," I said before Louise could tell Beatrice that Europe is across the ocean. Water is not a happy subject with us, and I wouldn't have Beatrice worried. I glanced up at Mother there on the wall, looking down on us from the frame and her grave. "They are going to Europe to find Olive a husband," I said. "They are going to marry Olive off."

"Is that what I was hearing?" Louise said, astonished.

"That's exactly what you were hearing," I said, because it was.

"But *why?*" Louise and Beatrice gibbered.

"Because no young man around here ever comes to call on Olive twice."

That was another true fact.

"You know yourselves, Mr. Cranston has looked as far as Rockland County for young men to call on Olive," I said. "Mr. Cranston has crossed the *river*, looking for a young man for Olive."

We stood sobered by the thought.

"And do we ever see any of them but once? No. They shy like horses and gallop off. The Cranstons will never get Olive off their hands by staying home. Olive is pushing twenty-one without a man in sight. And so they're going to have to try Europe." As soon as I said it, I knew I was right.

"Aren't the young men of Europe as particular as the young men here?" Louise wondered.

"As I understand it, they're not," I said. "Besides, in Europe, money buys everything. But with us, it's family that counts. *Family.*"

That was another true fact. I let it soak into Louise and Beatrice.

Then Louise said in a small voice, "Well, I hope it works out for them. I wouldn't miss Olive, particularly. As long as they bring Camilla back."

"Would they shutter the windows and shut up the house?" Beatrice said. "Then where would we—"

"We'll manage," I said. "Life will go on."

But I saw change coming, and that's always a worry, especially if you are the oldest.

Beatrice blinked hard at Louise. "Honestly, Louise, put on some clothes. You're home now."

And Louise, still muddled, looked around for her skirt and something for on top. When we are Upstairs, or out and about, we naturally wear nothing but our fur. We wear clothes only in our quarters, here within the walls. I make most of them myself and was wearing my apron with the frill. Beatrice was wearing her polished cotton, very girlish with the smocking across the bodice. But of course we don't dress like this when we're out someplace where we might be seen. How could we? We're mice.

WE ARE MICE, and as Mother used to say, we are among the very First Families of the land. We were here before the squirrels. The squirrels came for the acorns. We *sold* them the acorns.

And we were here ages before the Dutch came up this river. Ages. We made room for them, of course. They were well-known for their cheeses—Edam, Gouda—these Dutch people. And they built good strong stone houses, gabled and stout to keep winter out.

We came indoors then, in through the Dutch

We wear clothes only in our quarters, here within the walls.

doors. We came in from the cold and were field mice no more. We hardly needed our winter coats once we'd settled among the Dutch—behind their walls, below their floors, beside the Dutch oven. There were crickets on their hearths. But we were not far behind, gray as the shadows, between one loose brick and another. Here we hollowed out our homes. Just a whisker away, only a nibble from the cheese in their traps.

When they were Dutch upstairs, we were Dutch down here. We learned their tongue. We are excellent at languages. Excellent. And we took their names. I had an ancestress with a long gray tail and eyes as beady as mine, and her name was Katinka Van Tassel. How Dutch can you get?

After the Dutch came the English. Yes, the English, and very high and mighty. They brought taxation without representation. Tea—oceans of tea—and a ridiculous nursery rhyme called "Hickory Dickory Dock."

The English built a grander house around our Dutch cottage. And they cut the trees for a sunset view down to the river. Though water in any form is not a happy subject with us mice. The best reason for a river I can think of is for drowning cats.

But all of this was long ago, and our Upstairs humans are the Cranstons now, from Cleveland. And so we too are Cranstons, we mice, though of a longer tradition. We have the background they lack.

So there you have the history of our Hudson River Valley. A rodent view, naturally, and the short version.

"THEN I'D HATE to hear the long version," as my sister Louise always says. But that is Louise all over: snippy and skittery, though always first with the news, whether she understands a word of it or not.

We three were still there around the crumbed

table, dizzy with what she'd heard from Upstairs. Louise was fastening her skirt at the waist, though she has no waist. In the quiet you could hear something like thunder from high in the house.

It must have been Olive and Camilla and Mrs. Cranston running into each other as they tried on all their hats. It was the thunder before the skies opened to wash our old lives away.

Then our brother, Lamont, stormed into this thoughtful moment. Lamont—home in the middle of the day! Our hearts sank. Lamont— underfoot and everywhere you turned. His lashing tail swept two or three items off the shelves and the cheeseboard off the table.

Being a boy, he sowed the seeds of destruction wherever he was. And he was home now, hungry for his lunch because mouse school had closed at noon and all the scholars sent home. A cat had been sighted in the vicinity.

CHAPTER TWO

Skitter and Jitter

ALL MICE HAVE sisters, and you have met mine. I am Helena, the oldest. But I was once the mouse in the middle when it came to sisters. There were two older: Vicky and Alice. But they are no longer with us and can play no part in the great adventure coming in our lives.

Theirs is a painful story that we need not go into just yet. Mother is no longer with us either, which is part of the same sad story. As you may imagine, it involves water.

But now we needed to settle Lamont to his

lunch, or he'd pester us to death. Yesterday was baking day for the Cranstons' cook, Mrs. Flint. She has a heavy hand for pastry, but she bakes a passable corn bread. And a simple farmhouse cheese is not beyond her.

We lived in the kitchen wall, and our back door was a crack in the plaster nobody had noticed since the days of the Dutch. It opened behind the big black iron stove, just to the left of the mousetrap.

Mrs. Flint was an indifferent cook, but there were two good things about her. Her eyesight was poor, and she did not live in. Either she couldn't see us or she wasn't there. So we were pretty free to browse her kitchen for our meals.

And you may take my word for it: We had every right to our share. We were here first. Besides, mice can come in very handy to humans. Times come when mice more than pay their way. Just such a time was coming. Read on.

But now it was time to feed Lamont his lunch

of corn bread crumbled into a thimble of milk. We tied a napkin around his neck, for all the good it will do.

"Do not bolt your food, Lamont." I stood over him. Somebody has to. "Those teeth are for chewing. Think of the many mice who must forage for their food, Lamont. Mice who would be glad to be sitting at your place."

Lamont's stomach grumbled unpleasantly as he tore into his corn bread. His stomach is a bottomless pit.

Then this bothersome boy looked up, twitched his whiskers at us, and said, "Will they be taking Mrs. Flint with them when they sail for Europe? The Upstairs Cranstons?"

I slumped. Louise stared. At school Lamont learned everything but his lessons. How provoking that he'd heard the news as soon as we had. Maybe before.

"Sail? *Sail?*" Beatrice clutched her throat. "Is Europe across water?"

We were in a tizzy then until Lamont escaped out into his free afternoon. We barely got the napkin off him. He'd dropped down to all fours and scampered for the front door. He was half wild, was Lamont. Boys are.

"Keep one eye on the sky, Lamont," Louise called after him. Because any number of things can swoop down on a mouse. Things with wings and talons. Beaks. Especially upon a mouse who does not think. "And remember who lives in the barn!"

"And in the haystack," I added. Louise and I exchanged glances. What lived in the haystack didn't bear thinking about.

"Water?" Beatrice said in a strangled voice. "Europe is across water?"

CALM FINALLY SETTLED as we drew up chairs for *our* lunch, and a spot of coffee afterward. Mrs. Flint always left a pan of breakfast coffee at the back of the stove. We had a cunning little dipper we could send down into the pan on a length of picture wire.

We lingered over our coffee as the kitchen clocks struck, and then again. We are not good about time, we mice. For us, time always seems to be running out.

Then the front doorbell sounded through the house. We jumped.

Hardly anybody ever came to call. Mrs. Cranston and Camilla and Olive sat through long afternoons in their second-best clothes. They sat sideways on the settee because of their bustles, waiting for visitors who never came. They sat through whole dreary afternoons, corseted and alone.

The doorbell rang again.

"I'll go," said Louise, out of her chair, and her skirt. She could never wait to stick her nose into whatever might be happening.

"Curiosity killed the cat," I called out to her. This is one of my favorite sayings. Beatrice would have scurried after her if I hadn't given her one of my looks.

We sat on at the table, Beatrice and I. Mice hear better than humans. We should, with these ears. But only mere mumbling murmured down the house along the ancient trail in the walls blazed by mice before our time. We are a very old family, as I have said.

I kept Beatrice busy. Idle hands are the devil's workshop. Yes, we have hands. There is talk of paws and claws, but look closer. We have hands, very skilled. I can thread a needle while you're looking for the eye. I sew a fine seam, and Beatrice was learning. I tried to teach her what she'd need to know.

The kitchen clock struck another afternoon hour away. Which hour I do not know. We are not good with time. Through the wall Mrs. Flint's kettle sang. She was putting cups on a tray to send upstairs. I was beginning to wonder where Lamont was. I am the oldest, and so the worries reach me first.

But at long last a sound of skittering came from far up our front passage. Then nearer skittering and gasping mouse breath. We set aside our needlework, Beatrice and I, as Louise burst in upon us. Somehow it seemed that Louise was either just coming or just going. It was hard for her to settle.

"You'll never guess—"

"Skirt, Louise," I said. Beatrice handed it to her.

Louise stepped into her skirt. "Is there any of that coffee left? I'm dry as a—"

"You're keyed up enough without more coffee, Louise. Just watching you makes us jittery," I said. "You skitter and we jitter. Sit down and tell us what we will never guess."

She drew up a chair. "Where shall I start?"

"Who came to call?"

"Oh yes. A Mrs. Minturn." Louise made big eyes at us.

"Not a local family," I said.

"No, indeed. She came up from the city." Louise tapped the table. "On the *train*."

"Ah, if she is from New York City, she must be selling something," I said. "Everything is for sale in New York City."

"They showed her their hats, and she said they wouldn't do," Louise said.

"Was she selling hats?" Beatrice wondered.

"I'm not sure," Louise said. "She was wearing an awful old shovel bonnet herself. It was rusty with age, and so was she. And, oh my, her veils were torn."

"You seemed to get a good view of her, Louise," I remarked.

"I was under that marble-topped table by the horsehair settee, right at their feet. But they wouldn't have noticed me if I'd been sending up fl—"

"What was this woman's business, Louise? This sounds like business to me."

"Well, she was very businesslike," Louise

said. "But I'm not sure. She told them how they better dress if they were going to Europe. She said that bustles are over. Bustles are completely over in Europe. Nobody even remembers bustles."

"Then what?"

Louise pressed a finger to her cheek. "Oh yes, then she had Olive walk up and down the room. Up and down. Up and down."

"What for?"

"To see how Olive moved," Louise explained.

"How did Olive do?" Beatrice asked.

"Not very well. She ran into things and caught her toe in the rug. You know how Olive is around her mother. And Mrs. Cranston was jumpy as a cat. I was right there by one of her shoes, and she kept tapping it. She very nearly mashed me into the carpet. 'We must give Olive Her Chance,' she kept saying. Over and over like she does."

"How did all this end, Louise?" I asked,

"I was right there by one of her shoes."

because she was going on forever. "Put it in a nutshell."

"Money," Louise said.

"Money?" said Beatrice.

Louise nodded. "Mrs. Minturn said it would take money to unlock the doors of Europe. Nobody in Europe is interested in poor Americans. No young man is. Evidently they have enough poor people of their own."

We pondered all this. "Then what happened?" Beatrice said.

"Well, Mrs. Minturn just sat there with her hands in a bunch until Mrs. Cranston reached down for her reticule, which was just a whisker away from me. She handed her some money."

"How much?" Beatrice inquired.

"Well, how would I know?" Louise said. "She didn't show it to *me*. But it was quite a wad. What do you think this all means, Helena?"

The four eyes of my sisters fell upon me. But I was spared answering. Lamont exploded out of the front passage and was all over us. Lamont—flinging himself on the floor, right there on the rag rug. His eyes rolled like a mad horse. His underbelly showed pale as paper through his fur.

We were all on our feet. A chair fell over. A valuable chair.

Beatrice stifled a scream and pointed. "Oh, Lamont, where is the rest of your tail?"

CHAPTER THREE

The Haystack

WHERE INDEED? LAMONT writhed on the rag rug with far less tail to lash. The tip oozed. I couldn't tell how much was missing, but he had a stubby look. He was squealing till you couldn't hear yourself think. Somebody had to take charge, and I am the oldest.

"On your feet, Lamont," I said.

Louise wrung her hands. "Shouldn't we dip his stub into some rubbing alcohol or something? Don't we have ointment?"

"He is more scared than hurt," I said. "Up, Lamont."

He lolled and squealed, and I untied my apron.

"Where are you going, Helena?" Louise and Beatrice gibbered.

"Out," I said. "Lamont and I are going to get his tail back."

Lamont stopped in mid-squeal. Silence fell. He wouldn't meet my eye. He'd have slunk off to his room if he dared.

"Don't even think about it, Lamont. We are going for your tail. I hope you remember where you lost it."

Lamont cowered, but I marched him out of the room.

All the way up through the walls I bristled with things I felt like saying to Lamont, things he needed to hear. We turned into the passage under the Upstairs Cranstons' front hall. Our front door is a crack in the foundation under their porch.

We were outdoors then, under the porch. I was on all fours too, since you can move faster that way, and it's expected. When we crept out from under the spirea bushes, we were in open country, so we needed to keep one eye on the sky.

From the rear Lamont looked ridiculous without his complete tail. He paused and put a finger to his chin, though he has no chin. He was stalling.

"Which way to the tail, Lamont?"

I can read his mind. He considered leading me off on some wild-goose chase. But then he thought better of it and started through the grass around the side of the house.

Even when the grass is new-mown, we are up to our eyes in it. And it teems with beetles and earthworms and pesky ticks. Ticks are a trial to us. I was forever picking ticks out of Lamont's fur.

We rounded the house, and there was the rain barrel.

We turned away from it. Now down the slope

of the lawn the barn stood tall. We were making for the kitchen garden.

I was right on Lamont's heels along a row of spring onions. "Lamont, did you go in the barn?"

"Certainly not," he said over his shoulder, though he doesn't really have shoulders. "Gideon wanted to, but I said we better never."

Gideon. Of course. Gideon McSorley was a mouse a class or two ahead of him and Lamont's so-called best friend. Not a good influence.

"I notice that when you lost your tail, Gideon left you high and dry. He didn't see you safely home, though you were in a sorry state. Some friend."

But this is not reasoning a boy follows.

We were practically in the barn's shadow now. There was a whiff of horse, and something far more worrisome than that. "Lamont, are you certain—"

"Never went near the place," he muttered.

Only a fool would. A cat lives in the barn, to

keep down the vermin. And *we* are the vermin.

At one time there'd been a whole litter of cats in there, but only one remained. An old she-cat without a name. Barn cats aren't named.

It was this very she-cat who got Papa. Yes, our papa. In a scene too terrible to tell, she pounced. In the dust of the barn lot Papa had come across an ear of Indian corn. He could make a meal out of Indian corn and had just started through the second row of kernels when she pounced, all teeth and claws. I can't bear to say any more than that. Don't ask me.

That wicked old she-cat no longer has a tooth in her head, but she could gum you to death. I suppose if she caught you just right, she could get the tail off you. She was kill-crazy, of course. Cats are.

Past the barn, Lamont slowed to a stop. Now it was the haystack ahead of us—dead ahead, high and yellow.

"Lamont, tell me you didn't." I closed my eyes.

"Gideon said—"

"If Gideon said, 'Let us go down and fling ourselves into the Hudson River,' I suppose you'd do it. Oh, Lamont, you foolish, foolish mouse."

"Well, I won't do it again," he said in a squeaky voice. He was at the age when a boy's voice is especially squeaky.

"No," I said, "and you won't grow another tail either."

He wanted to turn back then, and who could blame him? Snakes live in the haystack. The haystack seethes with them. Poisonous snakes. Copperheads, and they are very active in the springtime after their long hibernation. It is said that copperheads are very shy of humans. But we are not humans. We are dinner, and the haystack was alive with death.

"We were just playing hide-and-seek," Lamont muttered. "Me and Gideon."

"Gideon and I."

"Gideon and I. Then over there by the hay-stack something clamped down on my tail. I shot away—like a rocket. I didn't feel a doggone thing. But when I looked back . . . there it was, starting to coil, with my tail in its mouth and its eyes staring."

A chill slithered down my spine.

"And where was Gideon then?" I inquired.

"Gideon said he was needed at home."

The haystack glowed golden in the setting sun. Lamont pointed. "Look!"

Right over there on the bald ground beside the lowest overhang of haystack, something—

"By golly, it's my tail!" Lamont flung himself forward.

Was it? Something was there, no bigger than a twig off a tree, and gray. Half a mouse tail is not a meal for a copperhead, but—

"Lamont, no!" I cried after him. "It's a trap!"

He skidded to a stop. I was on his heels. We were *this close* to that haystack, and our doom.

"It's a trap, Lamont, baited by your own tail," I cried. "Fall back, Lamont!"

But he wanted his tail, and we'd come for it. He squeaked a yearning little squeak. And my instinct took over. Something had to.

I cut and ran toward the haystack, pounding past my hapless brother. Onward I plunged till the whole world was haystack ahead.

At the last second, I swerved away, defying death and tempting the serpent. In that instant, a hideous head struck out of the overhanging straw—those unblinking eyes, those fatal fangs. How patiently that copperhead had waited. How wise of the copperhead to know that Lamont would be back for his tail. The wisdom of the serpent. But I am smarter. I am Helena, the oldest.

Jaws snapped on the air behind me, and a hiss shivered the barn lot. I'd practically served myself up for that copperhead's dinner, and all to give my brother a chance at his tail.

"Run for it, Lamont!" I shrieked, making a

At the last second, I swerved away, defying death.

large circuit of the barn lot. And here Lamont came, with the end of his tail unfurling from his mouth.

We ran till we couldn't, up the slope of the lawn. We were out of breath by the rain barrel, but that was no place to pause. In the shadow of the spirea we keeled over, gasping in the grass. But we could not tarry long there out in the open. The scudding clouds above us threw cat-shaped shadows across the yard.

"Lamont, this cannot go on. Even a cat has only nine lives, and we don't have that many." I was breathing hard. "I cannot keep saving you from yourself. The barn. The haystack. Where did you go as fast as you could scamper? Where, Lamont?!"

He hung his head. But he could make no answer, not with his tail in his mouth.

I MARCHED HIM home, and straight to my workbasket. Tying my apron about me, I rummaged for a needle and thread while Louise and Beatrice stood by, speechless. It was quite a long needle. All needles are long in the hand of a mouse.

"Bend over, Lamont," I said.

And I sewed his tail back on him, while he squealed the house down.

You do what you can. But I have to say, that tail never really worked right again.

CHAPTER FOUR

When Night and Darkness Fell

AFTER SUCH A day, how could I sleep a wink? Louise and Beatrice and I shared a bedroom just over our dining room. Lamont had his own room, hollowed out next to ours and very messy. I stared at the ceiling. If I dropped off, I'd dream. And mice dream about only two things: cheese and time running out.

Maybe I dozed, because floating there before my sleeping self was a giant wedge of Stilton cheese, richly pale against a red sunset. A lovely, creamy Stilton—blue-veined, so it was about six weeks old. But my sleeping self looked closer. It was no Stilton cheese at all. It was no such thing. It was the haystack in the last red glow of sundown. And lurking in that haystack: unblinking eyes and hovering heads and one scaly coil after another.

I trembled awake. Something besides fear had stirred me. I looked to the matchbox beside me, Louise's bed. There is nothing wrong with our eyesight. We see better in the dark than you do in daylight.

Louise eased back her scrap quilt and carefully, carefully slipped out of bed. She should know any little thing will wake me. I hardly sleep.

Her nightdress caught on her ears as she pulled it over her head. Now she was stepping around her chamber pot. It is a thimble with a dime for a lid. We have all sorts of uses for thimbles. That's why they so often go missing from the workbaskets of humans. Lose a thimble? I expect we have it.

Stealthy Louise lifted her tail to keep from knocking over anything as she made for the door. I knew where she was going. On her little mouse feet she was heading up the walls to Camilla Cranston's bedroom. Where else?

She'd shinny up the dust ruffle on Camilla's bed. Then she'd show her little pointed face there at the foot. And they'd have one of their midnight chats. I saw her with my mind's eye: Louise, listening, her tail arranged around her on Camilla's counterpane.

I knew where Louise went when night and darkness fell. And she knew I knew, and she knew I didn't like it. Of course, we're all family. They were Cranstons Upstairs. We were Cranstons down here. But nothing good comes of too much mixing. And it isn't fair. We understand their speech. They don't understand a word of ours. Not a syllable. We hear all about their joys, their sorrows. They hear nothing of ours. Nothing.

Besides, I had joys and sorrows to share with Louise. Why was that not enough for her? Why was *I* not enough? I stared at the ceiling, and all my worries crowded round my matchbox.

Lamont, naturally. Always Lamont, thoughtless with death at every turn. The haystack. The barn. The hovering heads. The pouncing cats. The brimming river and the busy road. The rain barrel.

I'd be worried into an early grave for trying to keep him out of *his*.

And now the Upstairs Cranstons, off to the ends of the earth, without a backward glance. Louise was bound to be lost without Camilla. Without Camilla she would droop and lose interest.

Two matchboxes over, Beatrice snuffled in her sleep. I say less about her, but she was a worry too. Meek to a fault was Beatrice. And though I didn't want to say it—a little bit mousy.

Wonder and worry like to crowd me out of my bed. But I may have drifted into a dream then. I must have, because there before my sleeping self rose an enormous sunlit Stilton cheese, seething with snakes.

But any little thing will bring me around. I heard a familiar skitter. Louise was back. She slipped under her scrap quilt. The night vibrated with her thoughts. She was all a-tingle, the way she gets.

She knew I never really sleep. "Well, it's all happening," she said, quiet because of Beatrice. "And sooner than we thought." She muttered near my ear. I felt the faint breeze of her breath. "They have ordered new hatboxes, and brought the steamer trunks down from the attic."

We pictured that: the steamer trunks being bumped down the stairs from the batty attic.

"They're to have new clothes from the skin out," whispered Louise. "As Mrs. Minturn said, they haven't a stitch that will do. Even corset covers. Everything. Seamstresses will come and sew night and day. The Upstairs Cranstons are going to London, England, and so they will need ball gowns. Even Mrs. Cranston."

Mrs. Cranston in a ball gown? I hoped she wouldn't show her bare shoulders to the world. They are very beefy, Mrs. Cranston's shoulders.

"Off they will go to the far side of creation," Louise sobbed slightly into my ear. "And leave nothing behind but empty rooms."

I did not reply, of course. What was there to say? Then Louise slept, and whimpered in her sleep. And there was I again with only my worries for company.

I tossed and turned on the human-hair mattress of my matchbox. Mrs. Flint suffered from thinning hair, and so there were always stray strands drifting around the kitchen floor—more than enough to stuff four mattresses. How handy we mice are for keeping things tidy. I would hate to think of the world without us.

She folded back her scrap quilt, and up she rose.

A thought occurred to me as it often does. Though I have my pride, it is not a foolish pride. I can go for advice when I need it—to Aunt Fannie Fenimore, of course. Where else? She was called the wisest mouse in both Westchester and Dutchess counties. Though she was no picnic to be around.

Still—once I'd made up my mind to go to Aunt Fannie, I may have drifted into a fitful sleep. I must have slept, because I seemed to dream. In this dream, Beatrice sat silently up, two matchboxes over. Beatrice! She folded back her scrap quilt, and up she rose, slipping out of her nightdress. Then she was gone like a puff of smoke.

But how could this be a dream since we mice dream of nothing but cheese and time running out?

CHAPTER FIVE

Two Futures

IT WAS ANOTHER busy week before I could
tear myself away for a visit to Aunt Fannie
Fenimore. Mrs. Cranston nagged Mr. Cranston until he had one of the new telephones
installed under the front staircase, where it
rang its head off. Another express wagon was
forever bringing up a parcel from off the train.
Bolts of fine silks. And cambric and lawn
for new petticoats, long ones and short ones.
Paper patterns. Buttons on cards. Skeins of
ribbon.

We were buried alive in all this newness that smelled of the shop.

A chattering, complaining army of seam-stresses fell on us, all sent by Mrs. Minturn. Pin-cushions on their wrists. Tape measures around their necks, and a welcome new supply of thim-bles. Then here came the tailors for Mr. Cran-ston's frock coat and morning coat and striped trousers and silk nightshirts with his initials sewed on. All these things he didn't know he needed.

Louise and Beatrice and I were up half the night every night, bringing down snippets of satin and serge that had fallen from the dress-makers' scissors. And ribbon ends. And any spool of thread, rolled under their worktables. And all the pins and needles worked into the carpet. Because you never know what you'll need. We think ahead, we mice.

Through the kitchen wall Mrs. Flint and her daughters moaned over all these extra mouths to feed. The tailors ate like horses. Mrs. Flint banged pans until you couldn't hear yourself think. But she made apple fritters for all, and we were up the other half of the night, bringing back all the peelings we could carry. We mice have a great use for apple peelings. They keep the curl in your tail.

Time was running out, Louise reported. The steamer trunks were crammed full. The luggage tags tied on. She'd come back with the news from Camilla's room, very droopy, tracking in cobwebs. Then she'd fling herself into her matchbox. She was very down in the mouth at the thought of losing Camilla to London, England.

AND SO I set forth on a visit to Aunt Fannie Fenimore. Into a cloth bag I could carry around my neck I folded my best outfit. And I stuck in a morsel of apple fritter wrapped in waxed paper. Aunt Fannie is very greedy. Don't go empty-handed to her.

For good measure, I brought her a scrap of watered taffeta from off the floor under a dressmaker. One of Aunt Fannie's nieces could make it up into a skirt and cape for her.

Because a visit to Aunt Fannie was always educational, I wanted to take Beatrice. But she'd made herself scarce that afternoon. And Louise was Upstairs, collecting ribbons and rumors. Lamont was at school. We hoped.

So I set off all on my lonesome, across the croquet lawn. The Upstairs Cranstons don't play. And no young man calling on Olive ever stayed long enough to finish a game. But it is important to have a croquet lawn. With one eye on the sky, I rested under a croquet hoop to catch my breath and rest my bulging bag.

The lawns were full of mice, coming and going. For every one of us you see, there are a thousand more. Ten thousand. But I had no time for idle chitchat. At least I didn't have to cross the busy road. Mice like us live in the big houses between the river and the road. And the Fenimores were the next house over, a hedge away.

Under their porch, I stepped into a new skirt, summery with sprigs. There was lace at my throat fixed with a glass bead. I looked nice.

The Fenimore humans were away. I crept down the silent house, inside the walls to Aunt Fannie's, dragging the sack along the narrow trail. It was well-trod. Mice come from all over to seek Aunt Fannie's advice. When I came to her door, one of her nieces—Mona—was barring it.

All mice of Aunt Fannie's years have nieces, and she used hers to fetch and carry for her.

Mona looked me up and down and saw my finery was new. She twitched. "Oh, it's you, Helena. I don't know if she—"

"Who is it?" Aunt Fannie cried out from the depths of her gloomy room.

"It's only Helena Cranston from across the hedge," Mona cried back. Aunt Fannie says she's deaf, though she hears everything.

"I've been expecting her," she bellowed.

She expects a lot. And she always claims she knows when you're coming. She claims she knows everything.

Mona led me forth into the dreary, hollowed-out chamber, into Aunt Fannie's presence. Her throne was an old cast-off powder puff. She sat on it, draped in shawls, though it was hot as August in here. You never saw an older mouse. She'd gone past gray to bald patches. Though she only had one tooth left, it was a big one.

Spectacles are rare on a mouse, except in some silly children's book. But Aunt Fannie wore a pair. They were made out of bent wire and chips of lens from a human's reading glasses. They seemed to work for her. I'll say this for Aunt Fannie: She sees better than she looks.

She gave me and my finery the once-over. "Humph," she remarked.

If I wanted any advice out of her, it was time for the presents. She stuck her nose in the apple fritter and handed it over to Mona, who was hovering. Mona hovers.

Aunt Fannie waited for more, so I drew out the scrap of watered taffeta.

She fingered it. "Not best quality. Somebody's been selling your Upstairs Cranstons short. Somebody's been taking advantage. What color do you call it?"

"It is changeable," I said, "back and forth between purple and green."

"I hope it's not for Olive Cranston," Aunt Fannie said. "It's all wrong for her coloring. Olive is sallow. And it's too grown-up for Camilla, being youngest. Camilla should be in white and pale pastels. Lavenders. Pinks."

Aunt Fannie is full of judgments.

"I believe it's for the mother, for Mrs. Cranston," I said. "A ball gown."

Aunt Fannie Fenimore grappled with her shawls. "Mrs. Cranston in a ball gown? I hope she isn't planning to show her shoulders!"

"You and me both," I murmured.

"Who is giving her this advice?" Aunt Fannie narrowed her eyes at me. Her lenses sparked.

"An old woman up from New York City on the tr—"

"The Minturn woman?"

I shrugged. You can't tell Aunt Fannie anything. She slapped her powder puff throne. Powder rose in the room.

"They have fallen into the hands of a crook and a fool. They would. She will put them in the wrong clothes and give them the wrong advice. She takes her cut from all the worst seamstresses and milliners and tailors in New York. And she's never been out of this country. She's lucky to be out of jail. The woman knows no more about how to behave in the Great World than a . . . McSorley."

Mere mention of this ragtag family from the wrong side of the road made all the nieces titter. Mona smirked.

I just stood there.

"The Minturn woman will sell your Upstairs Cranstons down the river. They are lambs led to the slaughter. They are not the first fools she's fleeced."

"I don't know what I can do about it," I mumbled. "They are packing to go this minute. The labels for first class are on the trunks. They're away across the you-know-what to marry Olive off. And leaving us high and dry. What can I do? What's to become of us?"

I let a note of pleading creep into my voice. This was to remind Aunt Fannie that I was only a poor orphaned girl with nowhere to turn for advice except—

"Well, you did right to come to me." She adjusted her shawls. "We must look carefully into both your futures."

Both futures?

"Everybody has two futures," Aunt Fannie said. "The future you choose. Or the future that chooses you."

She snapped her fingers in the dusty air. "Bring forth the crystal ball!"

Her nieces scattered in search of it. I sighed. I'd never been sure about that crystal ball. It was only a marble lost from some human child's game. An aggie. But Aunt Fannie swore by it.

Presently the crystal ball was before her, on its own pedestal. She made circles of it with her hands, and stared into its depths. I'd never believed in that thing, but now I wondered.

"Oh bother!" She looked aside. "It's going in the wrong direction. It's your futures we're worried about, but it's gone back."

The nieces were quiet as—mice. Mona hovered. I waited.

"Come around here and look, Helena. It's gone back to the past."

I edged around to gaze over her sagging old shape, into the crystal ball.

I staggered. There in the depths of the crystal ball was . . . the rain barrel at the corner of our house. Clear as day. It was winter, with a skim of ice across the rainwater. I couldn't face it. My hands were over my eyes.

"Never mind," Aunt Fannie said. "They've been fished out and given proper burials."

She meant my sisters, my late sisters, Vicky and Alice. Thoughtless girls who'd ventured out across the ice on the rain barrel on a fateful day of freeze and thaw.

And Mother, who obeyed all her instincts and scrambled up the barrel to save them. And was lost herself. All three drowned in the rain barrel. Time is always running out for us mice, and water often figures in.

Aunt Fannie thumped the marble. "I've been having trouble with this thing. It'll go in reverse, but I can't get it turned around to tell futures. Look there."

Though I dreaded another view of the rain barrel, I chanced a look. The crystal ball was crowded with humans in peculiar caps and wooden shoes.

"Oh for pity's sake," I said. "It's gone all the way back to old Dutch days."

"See what I mean?" Aunt Fannie pointed me to my place before her. "I wish I knew who to call to get it fixed."

She blinked through her specs and fingered her last whisker in thought. "Never mind," she said. "I can see one of your futures anyhow. The future that will choose you if you stay put and do not act. Not a pretty picture."

I worked my hands. Aunt Fannie's pictures were rarely pretty.

"For one thing, that brother of yours needs a firm hand because he's headed for trouble. He's wilder than the wind, and nagging him does no good."

"Well, I try not to nag him," I said, straightening my skirt.

"You nag," Aunt Fannie said. "We can hear you from here."

She missed very little. "Then there is Louise,"

she said hollowly. "Once the Upstairs Cranstons are off across the you-know-what in all
the wrong dresses, you will have Louise on your
hands. She is entirely too attached to Camilla
Cranston, and where does that leave you?"

Where indeed. Was Mona smirking? I
wouldn't look.

"Not to mention Beatrice." Aunt Fannie's
lenses glittered. Every niece listened. Mona's
hand stole up to her mouth.

Beatrice? "Well, I suppose I might have left
her in mouse school to finish her senior year," I
explained. "But she was learning nothing. Absolutely nothing. She doesn't know where Europe
is. And her mouth moves when she reads. I
thought I could teach her better than—"

"Schooling is the least of Beatrice's problems,"
Aunt Fannie said in a voice of doom.

No niece looked at me. They looked everywhere else. Their many eyes glowed in the
gloom.

"Beatrice is slipping out at night, as the whole world knows," Aunt Fannie said, "except you."

Beatrice? As in a dream I saw her creep out of her matchbox. Off she went into the night on tiny feet. What if it was no dream? What if it was the awful truth?

"Beatrice is seeing Gideon McSorley on the sly!" Aunt Fannie announced. Her nieces gasped at this . . . cat let out of the bag.

Lamont's so-called friend Gideon? A McSorley? I grabbed the lace at my neck. "We're lost." My voice broke. "And finished as a family."

"You can say that again," Aunt Fannie remarked, removing a single loose thread from her shawl.

I TURNED TO go, my mind blank, my eyes blurry. But then behind me Aunt Fannie said, "Ah, that's better." I looked back. Her nose grazed the crystal ball. Her specs gleamed. "Now we're getting somewhere. Here's your other future, Helena! Here's the one you can choose, if you dare."

I stood there, between one future and another. The nieces edged up behind Aunt Fannie's throne to glimpse the future I might choose.

"Ohhhh," they moaned.

Mona too. How provoking that Mona would gaze upon one of my futures before I myself. That moved me.

I elbowed her aside and peered down over Aunt Fannie's humped shoulder, into the depths of the marble.

No. Surely not. Anything but—

"There it is." Aunt Fannie tapped the crystal ball. "Plain as the nose on your face."

"I couldn't," I whispered. "We couldn't. How could we?"

THE MARBLE WAS awash, and water is not a happy subject for us mice. Stormy gray seawater crashed in waves. The marble filled to overflowing. Great, surging mountains and valleys of wicked water. I felt wet through.

A ship too big for the marble to contain.

Cutting through the seething sea was the sharp prow of a ship. A great iron ship, trailing black smoke. A ship too big for the marble to contain, rising and falling in the restless water.

My stomach rose and fell.

"Well, there you have it." Aunt Fannie thumped the dimming marble. Still, I caught sight of the light from row after row of portholes rippling yellow across black water before the marble went dark.

It was the great ocean liner carrying the Upstairs Cranstons to London, England.

"How wide is that . . . water?"

"It is called the Atlantic Ocean," Aunt Fannie intoned, "and it is just at three thousand miles across."

My sisters Vicky and Alice, and Mother too, had all been dragged to their dooms in a rain barrel not three *feet* across. Not *three feet*.

My throat was bone dry. "Mice don't cross—"

"Mice better," Aunt Fannie answered.

"But how in heaven's name?" I pled. "And how could I convince the others?"

Aunt Fannie adjusted her shawl. "That brainless brother of yours will welcome any reason to miss these last weeks of mouse school. He'd sooner drown than finish the semester."

True.

"And Louise would risk her silly neck to be wherever Camilla Cranston goes."

True, true. But Beatrice—

"And that boy-crazy Beatrice has kept Gideon McSorley a secret. She dare not refuse to leave him, or she will be found out!"

Aunt Fannie looked particularly proud of her reasoning.

Oh, I thought.

"There is nothing I wouldn't do to keep the family together," I said in a voice gone weak as ... water. "Nothing. After all, I am Helena, the—"

"Then you will have to go to great lengths." Aunt Fannie fingered a final whisker. "Great lengths indeed. Across land and sea, water and the world!" She shook a fist at the heavens. "A world of steam and humans and long, long distance!"

The nieces quaked and clung to one another.

She waved the crystal ball away. "Sit down, Helena, to learn what you will need to know."

All the nieces flopped right down and arranged their tails. They were agog and waited wide-eared to hear. So did I, of course.

But Aunt Fannie did a strange thing then. Mysterious. "Here is how you hold your family together," she said. Then she put out both her old hands, stretched wide open.

"That's how you hold on to family." She thrust her wide-open hands right at me. Right in my face.

But what could that mean? What in the world?

CHAPTER SIX

A World of Steam and Humans

WE SAILED AWAY to London, England, Louise and Beatrice, Lamont and I. We began our journey by steamer trunk—that biggest trunk that had stood open for days in Camilla's bedroom, filling up with her new finery. It had drawers inside.

We packed a morsel of food, for we little knew where our next meal was coming from. But we took not a stitch of clothes, as we had no luggage. Mice don't. Still, fur is perfectly suitable for traveling. Lamont naturally wanted to take everything he had. Boys collect things—anything useless. Lamont wanted to take all his collections: the birds' bones and the collar buttons and that ball of twine that kept getting bigger and bigger in his room. He was a regular pack rat, though smaller. "No, Lamont," I told him.

We sisters were to travel in the handkerchief drawer of Camilla's trunk, in among her sachets. Lamont went in the top drawer above us, in with Camilla's gloves and garters. It was the best we could do.

Before dawn, we swarmed up through the house, never daring a backward look. By the time the sun of that last morning crept across Camilla's sleeping form, we were hunkered, lurking within the drawers. Beatrice and Louise and I were nose to nose to nose, under the lacy edges of Camilla's handkerchiefs. It was a small drawer. There wasn't room to swing a . . . cat.

A scent of Mrs. Flint's coffee wafted up from the kitchen, and the house woke around us. Mrs. Cranston dithered up and down the hall. Mr. Cranston barked commands nobody obeyed. Olive and Camilla chattered from room to room as they seemed to be tying on their traveling veils and fur tippets. We lurked in our drawer, all ears.

What if Camilla reached in for a handkerchief at the last moment? We hardly breathed.

Then the men were there for the trunks. Rough hands slammed our trunk shut. We were all three dashed against the far wall of the drawer in a tangle of Camilla's handkerchiefs and the leftover apple fritter.

Above us, we heard Lamont bounce off every side of the glove and garter drawer. Beatrice clung to me. Louise braced both feet as we slanted down the stairs on some big bruiser's back. Then off the front porch and into the wagon bed. The Cranstons were traveling with a wagonload of steamer trunks. We sensed them piled around us, like coffins.

"Are we over water yet?" frantic Beatrice whispered before they'd had time to turn the horses.

A TERRIBLE DAY followed. We traveled at great speed and blind as bats. On and off express wagons. On and off the clanking train. Before we reached the gangplank at New York City, they dropped us once on cobblestones. We were knocked half senseless. One of my ears got bent and took forever to straighten out again.

Now we sensed water below. The damp crept in. Waves lapped the pilings. The blast of the ship's horn shook the world. We couldn't see a moment ahead. We couldn't see anything. Louise whimpered. Beatrice clung. I'd have taken my chances back home. Gladly. But you can't go back, not in this life. You have to go forward.

❖ ❖ ❖ ❖ ❖

AS NIGHT FINALLY fell, our trunk stood yawning open in Camilla's shadowy, swaying cabin. A band played in the distance. Bells rang. Whistles shrilled. All the humans seemed to be up on deck, watching us sail. But Camilla would be back soon, to unpack. Then what?

Then she was there, all over the cabin. She unwound her traveling veils and threw off her fur tippet. She unpinned her hat and rummaged in her jewelry case. We watched her through the crack in the drawer.

She was shortly down to her petticoats and pearls, and heading our way. We cowered as she searched through the hangers for her dinner dress. She pulled out the lavender one.

Beside me, Louise went to work, sorting through the handkerchiefs for the one embroidered with violets. She nosed it to the crack in the drawer. It would be the first one Camilla's fingers would find, and it went with

We watched her through the crack in the drawer.

her dress. She only had to open the drawer an inch, and the handkerchief practically popped out at her.

Camilla thrust it into the sash at her waist.

Now she was remembering she'd need her long white gloves. Gloves! She reached for the drawer above us. Imagine reaching for your gloves and getting a handful of Lamont.

The glove and garter drawer slid open. We braced for Camilla's screams.

But no sound came. Now she was at the mirror, pinching her cheeks for extra color. The pair of long white gloves lay draped with the fur tippet over a chair arm. One glove twitched. A furry ball, tightly furled, fell out of it. Lamont.

From somewhere a dinner gong sounded. Camilla was out of the door, pulling on her gloves. Camilla always had a pleasant, girlish way of darting about that Louise tried to copy.

We waited, all ears, as the Upstairs Cran-

stons gathered in the corridor outside. Skirts
sighed. Mr. Cranston grumbled. Mrs. Cranston
dithered, and her corsets creaked. And Olive no
doubt caught her toe in the carpet as they set off
for the first-class dining saloon. Olive was never
at her best around her mother.

Our drawer was still a little ajar. We peered
out. The electrified lamp above the dressing
table still glowed. There was nothing to dropping down, though there'd be no going back.
Somebody would be clearing out the drawers
and storing things in cupboards. They'd find
crumbs of apple fritter in our drawer. Heaven
knows what they'd find in Lamont's.

We dropped, and landed on our feet. We
always do. There on the carpet was Lamont, cool
as a cucumber, as if we'd taken ages. We huddled, and I tried to keep us together, but it was
like herding . . . cats.

We glanced past the trunk, around the flow-
ered chamber pot beneath the bed. The cabin

was small, nowhere near the size of Camilla's bedroom back home.

"At least she doesn't have to share with Olive," Louise remarked. "That would have made the trip endless for her. They'd be running into each other all the way across the you-know-what."

It was an elegant cabin with two portholes. The walls were paneled in satiny wood.

"At home we lived inside the walls," piped Lamont, stroking his chin, though he doesn't really have a chin. "Maybe we could—"

"Don't even think about it."

The voice came from above us. We jumped and reached for each other. It wasn't a human voice. It didn't blare or echo. It was more like one of us, but different.

"That's solid sheet metal you 'ave there behind the wood on them bulkheads," came the voice in rather an odd accent. "Good British sheet metal."

We looked up. Camilla's fur tippet stirred

on the chair. We were riveted. Two eyes, redder than rubies, looked down at us. Camilla's furs parted, and a head appeared, then an entire mouse, snow-white. A big mouse. Full-grown and then some, in the prime of life. Gorgeous whiskers.

Drawing up, he planted a hand on his big haunch and gave us the once-over. We must have thought we were the only mice on the Atlantic Ocean. But no.

He dropped down onto the carpet before us. He was light on his feet for his size. We sat back, upright. We were wearing only our fur, but that's what you travel in. The white mouse wore only his fur, but there was something official about him.

Beatrice, who had clung to me all day long, turned me loose. She gaped at this white mouse, who said, "'Ello, 'ello, what 'ave we 'ere?"

He had a funny way of talking. I found my tongue. Who else would? Louise's hand was clapped over her mouth. Beatrice was agape. Lamont was completely useless. I straightened an ear and spoke. "We are the—"

"Cranstons?" the white mouse said. "Party of four? Americans? Mister? Missus? Two young ladies? One pretty, one not-so-much? 'Usband-'unting?"

What? Oh—husband-hunting.

"Well, yes," I said, "and . . . party of four mice. We too are Cranstons, though ours is the older family. I suppose you are surprised to find mice traveling—"

"Nothing surprises me," the white mouse said. "I'll be your cabin steward. Call me Nigel."

We stared. Lamont stroked his missing chin with worry. Nigel was twice his size. The cabin lurched and rolled. We must have been out on the open sea now, the surging sea. But Beatrice didn't notice. All she noticed was Nigel.

"A . . . mouse steward?" I said faintly.

"You lot don't get out much, do you?" Nigel

"I'll be your cabin steward. Call me Nigel."

the steward said. "This is a British ship with British service."

Oh.

He loomed over us. "Whom do I 'ave the honor of addressing?" he inquired of me.

The . . . cat had my tongue. "Oh," I said. "I am Helena, the old—I am Helena. The boy is Lamont." I pointed him out.

Lamont cringed. Nigel looked down upon him.

"What went wrong with your tail, son?"

Lamont was trying to keep it out of sight since it was unsightly. "Snake got it. Sister sewed it back," he said, suddenly a man of few words.

"Ah well, these things 'appen," Nigel remarked. "You're not going to give me any trouble on this voyage, are you, boy?"

"Who, me?" Lamont squeaked, which was the best he could do.

"And this is my sister Louise." I nudged her.

Her hand jittered down from her mouth. "Pleased to meet you, I'm sure."

"And this is my sister Beatrice."

Beatrice was transfixed. "Pleased," she breathed. "*So* pleased."

Though nothing surprised Nigel, we seemed to. " 'Elena, Louise, Beatrice?" he said. "Where's Vicky and Alice, then?"

We liked to leap out of our skins. Even Lamont. Who was this magic mouse? How could he possibly know?

"How could you possibly know?" I said.

"As a matter of fact, I didn't," Nigel said. "But Vicky, Alice, 'Elena, Louise, and Beatrice are the five daughters of the Queen of England."

"You mean . . . humans?"

Nigel nodded. "Big ones. They are the daughters of 'Er Majesty, Queen Victoria, Queen of England and Empress of India."

Mother must have read that in a book. She was a reader. Perhaps it was meant to be that we were on this fateful voyage.

"Vicky and Alice are no longer with us." I

spoke in a hushed voice. "Nor Mother, of course."

"Ah well, for mice, time's always running out," Nigel said. "'Ooo's for a spot of dinner?"

THE WORLD IS a sudden place. How soon we'd fallen into the hands of this perfect stranger. Lamont gazed up at Nigel with hero worship in his eyes. And in Beatrice's eyes—just plain worship. Louise and I exchanged glances. We were at sea indeed.

There was nothing to getting out of Camilla's cabin. Mice can get under the tightest door ever hung. But there is more indoors to a ship than you can picture. The corridor ran to a dot in the distance past an endless line of cabin doors. We set forth, four gray shadows behind the white blur of Nigel's big backside and his commanding tail. We moved on all fours because it's quicker, and expected. From somewhere far off came the sound of a harp, so we were either dead or it was dinner music.

A fog of cigar smoke enveloped us as we passed the gentlemen's smoking room. And would you believe it? A fire burned beneath a marble mantel in there. A log fire snapping in a hearth here on the ocean deep!

As all the gentlemen had repaired to the first-class dining saloon, Nigel swerved inside so we could catch our breath. He drew up before the crackling fire. We followed and lingered by the fender, making a little group of ourselves. The fire felt warm on our ears. Firelight glittered in Beatrice's eyes. She was all eyes, this near Nigel.

There is something very comforting about an open fire. But then Nigel said, "You'll need to watch yourselves, you lot. Every minute, mind."

As if we wouldn't, thrown in under the very feet of all these hulking humans, ganged together with them within these metal walls. Honestly.

"There's a ship's cat," Nigel said in a hollow voice. "There always is."

We quaked. He had us in the palm of his hand.

Lamont ducked. We looked around the gentlemen's smoking room to see if a cat's eyes glowed from under the furniture, behind the damask drapes. You know cats' eyes—that sickening yellow. Louise squeaked.

"Oh, not now," Nigel said. "Not 'ere. 'E'll not give you any grief whilst I'm about." Beatrice looked up at Nigel, rapt. "'E won't tangle with *me*, the ship's cat won't. We've tangled before, and I closed one of 'is eyes, permanently. 'E gives me a wide berth. Still, when you're on your own, be on your guard. 'E's kill-crazy."

"Cats are," I remarked. Lamont turned in a perfect circle, looking in every shadow for a kill-crazy, one-eyed cat.

But now, warmed and warned, we continued our journey along the endless corridors.

Miles we went down the creaking ship, from one deck to another, following Nigel's tall tail.

Now we crept past the slick tiles of the Turkish bath. Very dank with clouds of steam. It was a whole world, this ship, and now we were in its very bowels. Surely we were below water level now, though that didn't bear thinking about.

THERE CAME THE worrisome smell of English cooking. We were *this close* to the doors of the kitchen—the galley—when they banged open. A line of enormous humans burst through and bore down on us. We skittered on the steel deck. Huge waiters in white coats carried trays of the dessert course, shoulder-high. Flaming puddings. I gave us up for dead. We'd been seen, and you dare never be.

The waiters clattered past us on their ringing heels. We were bunched beside the doors, trying not to gibber. Louise whimpered.

"We're doomed," I said. "They saw us. They certainly saw you, Nigel. You very nearly glow in the dark."

"He does," Beatrice breathed.

"'Course they saw me." Nigel stroked a gorgeous whisker. "But I 'ave me work to do, and they 'ave theirs."

"But—"

"Besides, at sea a steward outranks a waiter."

We gaped. "But you're a *mouse*." I was practically wringing my hands.

Nigel waved me away. "You're on British soil now, so to speak," he said. "Rank matters more than appearance."

We didn't know what to think, and the galley doors were still swinging. "Dinner is served," Nigel said. "Step this way, ladies, Lamont."

I MAY HAVE pictured us foraging for crumbs under the ship's stove for our dinner. How wrong I was.

The vast kitchens were a clashing of pans and far too many humans. We skirted it, moving through pantries to a storage room right at the end of the known world. We drew up by a tall pile of crated fruit. There in the shadows another shadow fell across us.

A mouse stood there: tall, gray, gaunt, very upright. Lamont ducked. This mouse before us carried a small towel, hemstitched, over one arm. At his neck was a neatly tied black bow tie. He and Nigel traded glances.

"How many?" The mouse looked far down his long nose at us.

"Four more for dinner, Cecil," Nigel said.

Four *more?*

"I suppose it might be managed," the gray mouse—Cecil—said.

"At the 'ead table, Cecil, if you please," said Nigel.

The *head* table?

Cecil looked even farther down his nose. His gaze just grazed us.

How shy we felt. Lamont crouched low.

"Perhaps it could be arranged," Cecil said.

And with a twitch of whisker and a nod of head, he led us around the crate.

On the far side we got the surprise of our lives. There sat easily a hundred and fifty mice, at three or four long tables—yardsticks supported by alphabet blocks. A hundred and fifty mice, at least.

A major infestation.

CHAPTER SEVEN

Dinner Is Served

A LOW CHEEPING SOUND of dinner conver-sation ceased. Three hundred eyes looked up at us newcomers. We hung in the glow of their gaze, embarrassed to death. We met so few new mice in our little life.

Cecil, the headwaiter, scanned up and down the yardsticks for somewhere to seat us. Young mice waiters with perky black bow ties bustled among the diners, stepping neatly over their tails, serving the soup course.

I know. I know. I couldn't believe it either.

"A great many mice travel with their 'uman families. The better families," Nigel explained. "Yank—American mice. British mice 'eading 'ome. We 'ave the entire chorus of *The Nutcracker* returning to the London stage. We're traveling full this trip, what with the Queen's Diamond Jubilee coming up."

Our heads whirled. Before we knew where we were, we'd been seated down at this end of a yardstick. Thimbles of a clear soup were set before us. As it turned out, we kept just a course behind the humans in the dining saloon above.

We must have thought we were the last of the latecomers. But like the crack of doom, the headwaiter's voice rang out: "All be upstanding for Her Royal Highness, the Duchess of Cheddar Gorge!"

The what?

A hundred and fifty mice pushed back from their yardsticks and rose to their feet. A hundred and fifty-four.

We'd been sitting on small spools. But next to me at the head of the yardstick was a miniature chair of English bone china, white with hand-painted rosebuds. The motto in gold on it read:

SOUVENIR OF SLAPTON SANDS

Cecil appeared, sweeping back the chair and dusting it off with the hemstitched towel. A mouse of a certain age strode up with the aid of a matchstick cane, gold-topped.

A Duchess? A royal one? How could she be? I never heard of such a thing among mice. But everybody at our yardstick curtsied or bowed. We did our best. She was seated right there at my elbow just a whisker away.

She wasn't as old as Aunt Fannie Fenimore, but she was getting there. A bit of bent wire seemed to be caught in the fur between her ears. A crown?

A mouse of a certain age strode up.

No, a tiara.

"We rarely dine in public," she announced in a carrying voice. "But we thought it might be amusing on the first night." She spoke just over our heads.

My land, she was grand.

She drew herself up, though she was rather bent. "I am Mouse-in-Waiting to Her Royal Highness, the Princess Louise, fourth daughter of the Queen. In the British Empire, Mice-in-Waiting assume a royal rank. It is tradition. Royalty has never made a move without their mice. We came over with William the Conqueror. My mother was a Roquefort. Who might you be?"

She observed me. Her teeth were terrible, and her breath would kill flies. But she was very sharp-eyed.

"I am Helena," I said, squeaking, petrified. "This is my sister Louise." I nudged her.

"Then that little shrinking creature on her

other side—the one before the boy—must be Beatrice." The Duchess of Cheddar Gorge indicated her.

Here we go again, I thought. "Yes," I said. "Vicky and Alice drowned in the rain barrel."

"How sensible of your mother to name you for the Princesses of the Royal Blood, the daughters of the Queen. It gives you something to live up to."

The Duchess leaned nearer me. Her breath took mine away. My whiskers drooped. "After a tour of the colonies, the Princess Louise and I are returning to London for the Queen's Diamond Jubilee. Sixty years upon the greatest throne in human history!"

My stars, I thought.

"And who are *your* humans?" Her whiskers were tangled and her tiara was rusty, but you better have an answer for her.

"Our humans are the Upstairs Cranstons, though we are the older fam—"

"Cranstons? Cranstons?" The Duchess gripped the bone china chair arm. "Mother, father, two daughters, one quite young, the other quite awkward?"

"Well, yes," I said. What a gossipy place a ship is.

"They have already made an unfortunate impression in the first-class dining saloon." The Duchess bent still nearer. "My dear, those dresses."

Oh, we were in over our heads now. Heads and ears. "But how could you know—"

"Our waiters overhear their waiters," the Duchess said. "The world is a much smaller place than it seems."

Her eyebrows rose high, though she didn't really have eyebrows. "And what is the purpose of their journey, these Cranstons? To attend the Queen's great jubilee?"

Everybody at our end of the yardstick was naturally all ears. "Well, I'm not sure they know about the . . . jubilee," I said. "They are 'usband—husband-hunting for Olive."

"They are off to a very poor start, I'm bound to say. They have fallen at the first fence." The Duchess shook her head. "Moreover they've picked the wrong ship. We are sailing very short of rank. There are only three unmarried Englishmen of title on the entire passenger list. Three only. I will name them for you. There is Lord Sandown, who will be the Earl of Clovelly. But he is presently only five years old."

Well, I don't suppose he'd do, I thought.

"And there is the Marquess of Tilbury, but he is eighty years old and has to be fed by hand."

Strike him off the list, I thought.

"That leaves Lord Peter Henslowe, who is twenty-four years old. But he's good-looking and will be hard to catch."

I was lost among these lords. "I don't think the Upstairs Cranstons are looking for a title for Olive. Lords? Earls? I doubt it, Duchess. They may not know what titles are. For Olive, they'd settle for just about any—"

"They have not set their sights high enough!" The Duchess tapped the yardstick. "They have not been well-advised. You have your work cut out for you."

We started and stared.

"You will have to take steps. You are their mice. Your fates are intertwined with theirs. You cannot leave important decisions to humans. Their heads are in the clouds. Times come when mice must pay their way. Your time draws nigh." She stared past me at Louise and even at Beatrice. She meant business.

We didn't know what to think. Our brains buzzed.

"How fortunate for you that you have met us," the Duchess remarked. "We take an interest in your situation. We can't think why."

She snapped a finger in the air, and three waiters nearly fell on her.

"Take away this soup!" she commanded. "It is entirely too clear!"

CAMILLA WAS ASLEEP when we came in under her door. Our dinner had run to twelve courses. The remains of the flaming pudding churned inside me. The night stretched before us.

The steamer trunk was gone, and Camilla's lavender dinner gown was wadded on the floor with all her underthings. She was tidier than this as a rule, but she may have had a miserable time in the first-class dining saloon. Louise crept over to examine the crumpled handkerchief with violets on it.

"I could sleep on her bed," Louise muttered. "She'd be glad to see me when she—"

"I wouldn't count on it, Louise," I said. I talked her into sleeping in the chamber pot under the bed. Beatrice and I went into Camilla's jewelry case. It stood open on her dressing table and was tufted inside. It was the best we could do. I wouldn't sleep a wink anyway, not this near a human. But I wanted Beatrice where I could see her.

You are wondering about Lamont? So was I. Nigel had taken charge of him. He spirited Lamont off to an airing cupboard he ran as a dormitory for traveling mouse boys.

"You've 'eard of the Boy Scouts?" Nigel had said. "They were invented in England. 'Ere at sea we've got the Mouse Scouts. My invention." Nigel jerked a thumb at himself.

"It's better to watch boys," he remarked, "and to keep 'em busy."

Lamont went gladly. Too gladly, if you ask me.

BEATRICE AND I lay curled in the jewelry case, in a loop of Camilla's pearls. They were the string her father had given her last year for her sixteenth birthday. How lumpy our bed was with all her lockets and bangles and her garnet ring. The hatpins were sharp. There was barely room for the two of us. Beatrice was asleep at once, breathing directly into my bent ear. What a provoking girl. The ship wallowed, and the ocean was a mile deep. She ought to be terrified. But she was sawing logs in my ear, and dreaming.

I can read her mind, tiny though it is. Mice dream of nothing but cheese and time running out. But she was dreaming of Nigel. She sighed.

Sea spray dashed at our portholes. Every rolling wave carried us farther from the only world we knew. I was almost homesick for the handkerchief drawer.

I may have dozed just lightly when an unearthly moan jarred me awake. All the fur on my body stood up. Then another moan. Human.

It was Camilla. I sat up. Beside me, Beatrice murmured, "Oh, Nigel, we mustn't," out of some ridiculous dream.

I peered over the lock on the jewelry case.

Camilla was struggling up in her bed, onto her elbows. She was in one of her flannel night-dresses. Her hair was a mess.

"Oh heaven help me," she said to the night. "I think I'm going to be sick."

The cabin tilted. The hangers in the closets clashed and tinkled. Unknown things rolled around the floor. Camilla was looking every-where for something to be sick into. She remem-bered the chamber pot and lunged for it.

Panic rose in my throat. What a shock for them both if she was sick all over Louise.

But in that instant, Louise bounded up on the foot of the bed, landing neatly. Camilla switched on her electrified bedside lamp. There was Louise, small as life, arranging her tail and cocking her little pointed face at Camilla.

"Eeeeek! A mouse!" Camilla kicked in the bedclothes, drawing up her feet and her sheet. She didn't know Louise from Adam's off ox. How could she? We were miles from home.

Louise lost her head and ran in circles, chasing her own tail. Which didn't help.

Except it did. Camilla was so startled, she forgot to be seasick. She was greener than a gourd, but she only swallowed hard. She lowered her sheet. Louise pulled herself together. They exchanged a long look up and down the blanket.

Camilla stroked her own cheek. "But you couldn't possibly be . . ."

Louise drew back on her haunches and rearranged her tail. She cocked her little face again at Camilla, trying to look exactly like herself.

"But how did you *get* here?" Camilla was thunderstruck. "How on earth?"

Louise thought. Then she sprang off the bed and scrabbled around on the carpet, out of sight. But you could hear her if you listened. Then she soared back up on the foot of the bed. She had Camilla's handkerchief in her teeth. It trailed behind her. The one with the violets. She nosed it forward for Camilla to see.

"My handkerchief?" Camilla's eyes widened. "You mean to tell me you came aboard in the handkerchief drawer of my steamer trunk?"

That was exactly what Louise meant to tell her. How well they seemed to understand each other. Louise tilted her little head and shrugged her shoulders, though she doesn't really have shoulders.

Camilla was hardly green by now. "Oh, Mousie!" she exclaimed, which seemed to be her name for Louise. "How glad I am to see you. Nobody else on this ship is friendly in the least."

They were soon into one of their murmuring, one-sided conversations. As if they'd never left home. As if I wasn't right here in this jewelry case, just out of earshot.

I am too proud to eavesdrop, and so I could only wedge myself into the pearls, avoiding the hatpins, with Camilla's garnet ring gouging into my back and Beatrice's nose in my ear.

They were soon into one of their murmuring, one-sided conversations.

"Oh, Nigel," she murmured from deep in a dream, "do we dare?"

How I longed for home then. Our old home in the kitchen wall behind the stove, in our matchboxes with the scrap quilts and the human-hair mattresses.

I had led us away from all we knew in order to keep us together, to be family. Now look at us.

Louise (*Mousie!*) and Camilla as if I didn't exist. And Beatrice, who was either terrified, lovesick, or sound asleep. And Lamont gone gladly off into the unknowable world of boys. Mouse Scouts indeed.

I am Helena, the oldest, I reminded myself in the dark of that night. But I felt like Helena, the only.

I could have wept.

CHAPTER EIGHT

The Law of the Sea

THERE IS NOTHING restful about an ocean voyage.

At first light Louise's shadow fell across our jewelry case. "Rise and shine, you two. They'll soon be bringing Camilla's breakfast."

Very bossy.

Where were we three to go from here but under the bed? It was dusty down there. The English spit and they polish, but they do not dust. Beatrice sneezed.

The breakfast came, on a table with wheels.

The waiter's big shoes were *this close*. I never could get used to being so near humans. Never. They are simply enormous. The maids burst in, and they were all over the cabin.

"What are they doing?" I muttered to Louise.

"They are laying out Camilla's clothes," she muttered back. Hangers clattered. "It is a scandal that she and Olive and Mrs. Cranston aren't traveling with their own maids. Everybody says so."

Their own maids? We recalled Mrs. Flint's daughters. They'd have been hopeless at sea. They weren't that much use at home.

Bedsprings squeaked above us as Camilla struggled upright. The door fanned, and humans came and went. My stomach flapped lightly against my backbone. I thought I'd never be hungry again after that dinner last night, but I was.

Then a human hand reached down, very near us. It was Camilla's, thrusting a small plate under the bed, right in front of us. A point or two of toast, buttered. A small mound of scrambled egg. A morsel of bacon and two grapes. Louise's breakfast, courtesy of Camilla. There was enough for three.

BREAKFAST WAS NO sooner over than the maids were back, pulling Camilla's traveling coat out of the closet, lacing up her shoes for her, rummaging for hatpins.

"Now what?" I murmured to know-it-all Louise.

"They are dressing her for the deck and putting her life preserver on."

My heart nearly stopped. "Are we *sinking?*"

Though I whispered, Beatrice was all ears.

Louise rolled an eye. "It is a lifeboat drill. All the passengers report to the open deck and stand by the lifeboats to be counted." Louise looked very superior. "It is the Law of the Sea." She preened.

"Well, excuse me for not knowing, Louise," I snapped. "We don't all have humans to tell us things."

I sniffed. Louise sniffed. Beatrice was still all ears.

Bells rang. A whistle shrilled. Camilla and the maids swept out of the cabin in a flurry of skirts.

A little peace and quiet at last! I hadn't drawn an easy breath that near humans. I never do. But busybody Louise was already making for the door, peering under it out to the crowded corridor. Though curiosity killed the cat, Beatrice and I followed. We could barely see above the pile in the carpet, but the Upstairs Cranstons were all out of their cabins, jostling each other and retying the ties on their life preservers.

Mice rarely laugh, but I was tempted. Over their heaviest outdoor clothes they wore great, bulky, bulging things strapped around them. Mr. Cranston, a large, shapeless man anyway, in a bowler hat and his windowpane plaid great-coat under his life preserver. Mrs. Cranston, bigger than he, in a gigantic feathered hat, her squirrel-skin cloak, and over that her life preserver, stretched to its limits.

"She'd sink like a stone," Louise muttered in my ear. "That life preserver wouldn't float her *hat*."

Olive looked wretched. She'd anchored her hat with a pea-green veil that matched her face. She swayed sickeningly. Camilla looked the best of them as she always did. But a life preserver is flattering on nobody. Law of the Sea indeed. They looked ridiculous.

Mrs. Cranston fussed over them all in that way she has, but they were heading off along the corridor to the open deck. I was just ready to duck back inside the cabin when I got a shock more surprising than I can tell you. Beatrice and I were cheek by jowl under the door when out of the blue she blurted, "Well, I for one am not going to be left behind! The Upstairs Cranstons are heading for the lifeboat! I'm going too. We are their mice. Our fates are intertwined with theirs!"

I was so stunned by this outburst I could hardly utter. "Beatrice, it's only a lifeboat drill. An *exercise.*"

"You don't know that," Beatrice babbled right in my ear. "It could be the real thing! Besides, I bet ships have sunk before during lifeboat drills. You know nothing about it. You don't know everything, Helena."

She was hysterical. I would have slapped her, but there wasn't room. "Beatrice, they are making for the open deck," I explained. "It will be miles and miles of ocean in every direction. You'll be petrified. It's *water*, Beatrice."

"I don't care," she said. "I want to see that lifeboat with my own eyes. You never know if we might need it!"

And with that, she squirmed under the door

and shot off down the corridor before Louise or I could think.

We watched round-eyed as she bore down upon the dawdling Upstairs Cranstons. There's nothing wrong with our eyesight, and we saw her take a flying leap at the dangling tails of Mrs. Cranston's squirrel cape. She was swallowed up by squirrel tails and distance.

We were shocked witless. Our chins would have been on the floor except they already were. Then into my other ear Louise muttered, "She might have a point."

"What?"

"She might. I wouldn't mind knowing where the lifeboat is. Besides, it didn't take Beatrice long to infest Mrs. Cranston's fur cape. What will she get up to next, do you suppose?"

Then we were both squirming under the door and flying along the corridor. Our feet hardly grazed carpet. Louise was in the lead. I tried to keep up, but I'd had so little sleep. You try spending the night on a mattress of hatpins and pearls.

I could see Louise closing the gap between herself and the sweeping skirts of Camilla's coat—a gabardine duster.

And that's all I saw.

Just ahead of me a cabin door opened. Two gigantic human figures stepped out—men. Right in my path. The whole world before me was a dark herringbone tweed. I tried to stop. I tried my best. I did a complete somersault and went whiskers over teacup, ending up on my back, facing the wrong way.

Now panic gripped me. I scrambled up. But I could see nothing of the Upstairs Cranstons or Louise. I could see nothing but gentlemen's boots and trouser legs. I leaped onto the trouser leg of the second man. Pure panic, and not a good place to be if he followed the other man off down the corridor.

But above me he spoke. "Oh, sir, I quite forgot

your lap robe," he said. "You may require it on the open deck."

"Very well, Plunkett," said the other man.

With that, he—Plunkett—turned back to the cabin door. He strode inside, and I swung like a bell from his trouser without the sense to drop off. Besides, he could have mashed me into the carpet *like that*.

The cabin smelled of bay rum aftershave lotion. The lap robe was a blanket in the ship's colors, with fringe. He reached for it. I reached for the hem of his overcoat. Then I was traveling. You can get your nails into herringbone tweed.

I swarmed up him, over the life preserver, spongy with all its milkweed inside. Now I was on one of his tweedy shoulders. If he'd glanced sideways, we'd have been eye to eye. This was no place to tarry.

I was right by Plunkett's ear, in the shadow of his bowler hat. I looked up. A short leap and a little luck, and I could swing up into his hat brim. Panic propelled me. There are forces stronger than gravity.

Up I swung and lit in his brim. It was a curly trough around the crown of his hat. I settled in, very supple. Of course, I was six feet off the deck on the head of a human—a perfect stranger and probably foreign. What a sudden place the world is.

Out in the corridor my human kept a step behind the other man. Now we were on stairs. Now a heavy door swung and a sharp gust of damp ocean air hit us. Plunkett's enormous human hand came up to grab the brim of the hat, trapping one of my whiskers.

I hadn't thought of this, of course. I hadn't thought at all. What if this bowler hat blew off his head? I lay in the trough of the brim, paralyzed. What did I fear more, those four fingers, big as giant sausages, gripping the brim and my whisker, or sailing off his head and out to sea?

It wasn't a long walk to our lifeboat. By now I'd figured out that I was in the hat brim of a servant. Ladies travel with their maids, as everybody knows. I supposed gentlemen traveled with their valets, or whatever persons like Plunkett were called.

Humans milled just below me. I hazarded a look over the brim. There upon the crowded deck was an ancient human in a flat cap and many lap robes. In his life preserver he looked like a beached walrus. He slumped in a wheelchair pushed by his valet. The Marquess of Tilbury, no doubt, who had to be fed by hand.

Then out of the milling throng came another pair of quite a different kind, though also English. Striding along the deck was a woman, treetop-tall with the face of a disapproving prune. On her head a starched cap, with veils flowing down her back. A very superior servant, no doubt. A nanny, in fact, because attached to one of her hands was a small boy, in a sailor cap with ribbons. Well, not small, but about five years old in human terms. He carried a rubber ball that he wouldn't be parted with even for boat drill. In fact, he looked like a rubber ball himself, wearing a life preserver.

His small blue eyes were nearly lost above his enormous pink cheeks. He wore a sailor suit to go with his cap. His shoes buttoned up his fat legs.

Here was undoubtedly little Lord Sandown, who would one day be the Earl of Clovelly. He looked like he might be a handful. But the nanny gave him a sharp jerk to keep him near her serge skirts.

I chanced a look beyond him, and there was . . . the sea. More water than I knew there was. Gray and choppy. A world of water. The deck rose and fell. The lifeboats swung from their davits. I hoped in my heart we'd never have to get in one of those things.

Whistles shrilled. Uniformed men tried their

best to round up the humans to stand near their lifeboats and be counted. But it was like herding you-know-whats.

My two human gentlemen stood a little apart from the crowd. The other gentleman spoke. "I shall not be needing the lap robe, Plunkett, on such a pleasant day at sea."

He was quite nice-looking for a human, and young in human years.

"Very good, Lord Peter," said my human— Plunkett.

I nearly forgot my fear, there in the brim, staring at sky and trailing smoke. Lord Peter? Could this be the Lord Peter Henslowe the Duchess of Cheddar Gorge had named at dinner last night? Twenty-four years old and good-looking and hard to catch?

What strange fate had brought me so near him, I wondered, in all this multitude of humans?

I chanced another look. Beyond Lord Peter's

I chanced another look.

fine profile I saw all the Upstairs Cranstons in a clump. Sea breeze whipped Mrs. Cranston's hat into a frenzy of feathers. I scanned her for Beatrice. But no saucy, beady eyes appeared to peer out of her squirrel pelts. And while Louise must have been someplace on Camilla's person, I couldn't see where.

As I watched, Olive detached herself from the family and staggered on the slanting deck to the railing. There she was stupendously sick over the side of the ship. Oh my, she was sick. It went on forever. I hoped there were no people leaning on the rails of lower decks.

Her family rushed to her aid, to keep her from pitching over in that space between the rail and the lifeboat.

"Let me go!" Olive announced. "I'm dying anyway." She threw her head over the railing yet again.

"Olive has not found her sea legs!" Mrs. Cranston boomed to the world. "Send for the doctor!"

"Plunkett," Lord Peter said quietly, "give the young lady my lap robe."

Plunkett and I surged forward. I cringed in his brim. Now Olive was sagging in Mr. Cranston's big fists. She hung there, pea-green, with her damp veils plastered against her preserver and her hat over one ear. She wasn't dying, but she was willing. And she looked her absolute worst.

"Sir, for the young lady," said Plunkett, holding out the lap robe for Olive's heaving shoulders.

"Good of you," Mr. Cranston rumbled. Mrs. Cranston loomed up to wrap Olive in the lap robe.

I should have seen this coming. I should have thought ahead. Why didn't I? In the presence of a lady, even Mrs. Cranston, Plunkett . . . reached up to take off his hat to her.

The giant sausage fingers appeared again, to grip the brim. Off came the hat. My world tipped and tilted. I skidded halfway round the trough. Then I was in the air, turning there above the sea and the lifeboat and the slanting deck. I seemed to soar somehow. I scudded like an autumn leaf, grappling with thin air. I lit directly on the ship's railing. We always land on our feet, but another inch in the other direction, and I'd have gone straight into the sea and fed myself to the fishes. Water is not a happy subject with us mice.

The air was knocked out of me. But I gripped the railing, fighting for breath, pulling myself together.

Honestly, what a day.

A murmur went up. I had appeared from nowhere. Now I was in plain sight where you never want to be. Dozens of humans were astonished to see me there. Scores of humans. I felt their eyes. "Eeeek," said several.

"Floyd!" Mrs. Cranston clutched her husband and shrieked. "The rats are deserting the ship. We must be sinking!"

"Fiddlesticks, Flora," roared Mr. Cranston. Olive still sagged in his hands. "It's only a mouse."

"Oh, Mousie!" Camilla exclaimed.

It was time I made tracks. But the railing was slick with polish. The English spit and polish. I scrabbled and skidded. I slipped sideways. Sea breeze caught my ears. My tail was all over the place. I might yet pitch into the unforgiving sea. I looked in that direction, into the lifeboat.

I froze. There on a bench, sitting in orderly rows, were easily twenty mouse boys. Mouse Scouts. Standing over them was Nigel, taking roll. They too were having lifeboat drill. They all looked up in surprise at me, though nothing surprises Nigel.

I didn't pick out Lamont from among them. I simply didn't have the time. I ran for my life.

CHAPTER NINE

A Royal Command

PURE PANIC HAD sped me out of Camilla's cabin. Instinct led me back. Now I
lay panting under her bed, planning never to
budge until we docked. Exhausted. My head
rattled with all I'd been through—the tipping
hat brim, the endless sea, all those humans.
From the cabin next door came Olive's piteous
moans and a deep voice. The doctor must have
arrived.

Though I didn't mean to blink until Beatrice
and Louise were back, I dozed off and dreamed

that I'd missed the railing and was feeding myself to the fishes. A dream of time running out.

Voices brought me to the surface. "Oh for pity's sake, Helena. Napping in the middle of the day?"

Louise was back, and with her Beatrice. Beatrice sneezed.

"That squirrel cape of Mrs. Cranston's is disgusting," she said. "It reeks of mothballs and camphor and . . . squirrel. I like to have suffocated."

I gathered myself up and did something with my tail. I had hardly slept. "But what about the *sea*, Beatrice?" I said with my usual concern. "Weren't you terrified?"

"I never really saw it," said the provoking girl. "I couldn't fight my way out of all those dead squirrels." Beatrice pondered. "Oh, I did just manage one peek. I saw you on the railing, Helena. Honestly, what were you thinking?"

I would not dignify that question with a reply. I turned to my other sister. "And where were you the whole time, Louise? I looked and looked."

"I was in the patch pocket on Camilla's duster coat, just under the life preserver. I could see everything. Really, Helena, showing yourself to all those humans! When Mrs. Cranston began screeching about rats deserting the sinking ship, I was so embarrassed I didn't know which way to look. I'm surprised some human didn't fold up a newspaper and give you a good swat."

We were nose to nose to nose under the bed. I bristled, but refused to explain. I have my pride. Besides, we were interrupted. A commanding voice came from the door.

"'Ello, 'ello, anybody at 'ome?"

We goggled at each other. Beatrice quivered.

"I 'ave 'ere an invitation from 'Er Royal 'Ighness, the Duchess of Cheddar Gorge, Mouse-in-Waiting to the daughter of 'Er Majesty Queen

Victoria. She commands your company for tea this very afternoon!"

We gaped. Then we ran squeaking into one another. Then we emerged from under Camilla's bed, all agog.

And there before us stood . . . Lamont.

Lamont!

He sat back on his spindly haunches with his hand propped on one of them. He was trying to be as much like Nigel as he could manage. Oh, how hard he was trying.

"Lamont," we demanded, "what are you saying, and why are you saying it like that?"

He preened. "I 'ave the honor of being Nigel's new assistant cabin steward." 'E picked me over all the others! We are a team, me and Nigel!" He preened again.

"Nigel and I," I said.

"Nigel and I. And you three are wanted for tea with the Duchess at quarter past four o'clock sharp." Lamont stroked one of his sparse whiskers as if it were one of Nigel's gorgeous ones.

But why in the world would the Duchess want us for tea? We asked this.

"It's a Royal Command," said Lamont down his nose. "Ours is not to reason why. Ours is to turn up on time."

"But how will we know when it's quarter past four o'clock?" Beatrice said. She had a point. We mice are not good with time. For us, it's always run—

"The gong will sound at four o'clock to summon the 'umans to their tea in the Winter Garden," said Lamont, who was 'ardly—hardly Lamont at all. "Once they're out of the way, then you three 'ightail it for the Duchess's suite."

"But where—"

"I shall meself conduct you," Lamont said grandly. "Now, if there are no further questions, I 'ave other duties. Nigel keeps me on the 'op."

Then he was under the door and gone.

We gazed at where he'd been.

"Why don't boys ever want to be themselves? Why do boys always want to be somebody else?" asked Louise, who wanted to be Camilla.

"How can we go to tea like this?" Beatrice said. She looked down at herself.

"Fur is perfectly correct for travel," I pointed out.

"For tea with a Duchess? A royal whatever?" Beatrice said. "I doubt it. I doubt it seriously."

Provoking girl, but she had a point.

At quarter past four o'clock, probably, we were at the Duchess's doors with our hearts in our mouths. Know-it-all Lamont had led us up and up through the ship to this very grand deck. The carpet was thick. The brass work gleamed like gold.

The sounds of a string quartet echoed up from the Winter Garden. The humans were having tea there. Not Olive, of course. Olive was in bed.

Still, we'd darted and scurried the whole way and hoped not to be noticed. After all, look at us.

There was Beatrice in an elegant skirt of Swiss cotton, a handkerchief folded and gathered at the waist, though she has no waist. And look at Louise, in Camilla's handkerchief with the embroidered violets, flounced, and a high Empire waistline. And I in white linen with a crocheted pink border, which is right for my coloring. We looked nice.

Following Lamont's patchy tail, we went in under the doors. It wasn't easy in these skirts. On the other side in the Duchess's front hall stood a very small mouse, hardly life-sized. She was hip-deep in the carpet and then some.

"What names?" she inquired.

"The sisters Cranston," Lamont said, " 'Elena, Louise, and Beatrice."

The undersized mouse wrung her hands. "Oh, I shall never remember all that."

"Never mind." Commanding Lamont waved a hand. "I'll announce them. Show us the way to the Duchess!"

How he got all this training in a single day I'll never know. He may have learned better away from school. Besides, he wanted to be Nigel.

We crept into the drawing room on all fours, not easy in these skirts. Beatrice tripped herself up and nosed into the Persian carpet, twice. The furniture was overstuffed cut velvet with tassels. The paneled walls were hung with paintings of female humans swinging in beribboned swings. So this was how royalty traveled. You wouldn't know you were at sea. The room hardly swayed. A fire snapped and crackled in the marble hearth.

Before it, outlined in flame, the Duchess of Cheddar Gorge, Mouse-in-Waiting to the daughter of the Queen, leaned upon her matchstick cane with the gold top. Firelight burnished the tiara between her ears. The room was enormous around her, but she filled it with her being.

"The sisters Cranston," Lamont announced in a piping voice that crackled like the fire. "'Elena, Louise, and Beatrice.

"Curtsy," he muttered, as if we wouldn't. We dropped three curtsies. We did our best.

Lamont withdrew. The Duchess looked us over. She was shaky on her pins, but sharp-eyed. "What pretty skirts," she deigned to say, looking away.

Beside her on the brass fender of the hearth a tea was laid out: steaming thimbles and a variety of crumbs; tea cake and crumpet and cucumber sandwich, on polished British pennies. Bits of cheese, a creamy Bel Paese, tastefully arranged.

We had soon settled on the hearthstones, the fire warm on our faces. Our skirts collapsed picturesquely around us. The undersized mouse and two more like her moved among us, serving us our tea. It was excellent. My crumb of tea cake had a raisin in it.

It took the Duchess no time at all to come to

the point. "We shall explain the circumstances of our household," she said over a thimble. "In addition to ourselves, Her Royal Highness Princess Louise is attended by a human lady-in-waiting, Lady Augusta Drear. They naturally do not take tea in the Winter Garden. We rarely partake in public. At present the Princess is being kneaded in the Turkish bath."

We stared.

"She is having a massage," the Duchess explained, "and Lady Augusta is holding the towel."

My stars, we thought. This is certainly life at the top.

"We live quite differently at home, when we are In Residence," the Duchess continued. "We would hardly have our tea off a fender and pennies there! We have our own fine doll china in our quarters within the palace walls."

We stirred.

"Buckingham Palace."

The Duchess looked wistful at the thought of home. "Are there any questions?" Her missing eyebrows rose high. Her eyes sought me out. I felt special. As this was something like school, I put up my hand.

"Yes, my dear."

"Only one question, Duchess. Does the Princess Louise, daughter of the Queen, *know* you are her Mouse-in-Waiting? Does she acknowledge your presence?"

The Duchess looked pensively into the fire. "She does and she doesn't. To royalty, all the rest of the world are rodents in a manner of speaking. As for her lady-in-waiting, Lady Augusta Drear, *she* is mortally afraid of mice. And so I must exercise all my tact as I go about my duties."

We tried to take in all this information, and the cheese.

"That brings us to the purpose of this tea," the Duchess said. "We dare not tarry, as the servants will soon be back and the Princess and

Lady Augusta will be returning from the Turkish bath. Time is short. But then, time is always running out for mice, don't you find?"

We did.

"Certainly Lady Augusta must not discover us in plain sight having tea off the fender. One mouse sends her into hysterics. Four mice, three of them in skirts, would send her overboard into the open sea. She is high-strung."

The Duchess set her thimble aside. A small mouse maid whisked it away. The other two were already clearing the fender of pennies. Good little workers, all three of them, though I don't suppose they dusted.

The Duchess cleared her throat. "It has been brought to our attention that your human Cranstons have not had a good day at sea. We understand that the older daughter is a poor sailor. And the mother was heard to cry out that the ship was sinking during lifeboat drill. This shows a great lack of tact. In fact, none."

How true.

"The family is not using their time at sea to meet the right people. Apart from the ship's doctor, they don't seem to be meeting anybody at all."

They wouldn't. The Upstairs Cranstons never were very good mixers.

"This is an opportunity tragically lost," the Duchess declared. "How important these ocean voyages are when people are thrown together. Dynasties have been decided. And so we must take steps. It is all for the sake of family."

And that, of course, is a thing I've always believed.

The Duchess was already hobbling across the carpet to a fine writing desk, probably Chippendale. Firelight glowed in its polish and winked on its brass drawer pulls. We followed. At the desk's elegant feet, the Duchess looked up. You could hardly see to the top.

"My leaping days are over," she said with feeling. "And my climbing days are coming to a close." She took my arm and drew me near. "You will have to help me up those drawer pulls to the top, my dear."

Ours is not to reason why. It took all of us to get her there. I went first, pulling her from drawer pull to drawer pull as the Persian carpet fell away below us. Beatrice and Louise boosted her from behind with her tail all over their faces. None of this was easy in these skirts. The Duchess carried her walking stick in her teeth. She was a game old thing.

We were no sooner at the cluttered top than she got busy, hobbling over the blotter, swerving around the inkstand. "Now, where is that guest list?" she wondered aloud. "I know Lady Augusta was working on it only this afternoon. Ah!"

She nosed a sheet of cream-laid paper our way. The names on it were written in a flowing script.

"I will explain. Her Royal Highness the Princess Louise will honor a very few of her fellow passengers at an evening reception in the near future. A little music and light refreshment."

We stared, mystified.

"One of our several talents is that we can copy the Princess's handwriting," she said. "Being artistic, she writes in a beautiful script. So do we."

"Oh for pity's sake," Louise blurted. "She's going to invite the Upstairs Cranstons to the Princess's reception!"

We gasped and goggled. The Duchess nearly smiled. We glimpsed her terrible teeth. "Ink," she ordered, "and a pen."

EVEN GETTING THE lid off the inkstand was a job. And you should have seen the pen in the Duchess's hand. It was like writing names with a telephone pole.

But, oh, she was deft. With her old bent back crouched over the page, she wrote an artistic hand. Her letters had loopier tails than her own.

Oh, she was deft.

Each time we three carried the pen back to be dipped in ink, she ran a hand down the arch of her aching back.

But the names emerged, drying upon the page:

Mr. and Mrs. Floyd Cranston
Miss Olive Cranston
Miss Camilla Cranston

It was not the work of a minute, and time was running out. Handing the Duchess back down from one drawer pull to another was no picnic either. And her breath like to take the finish off the desk.

But we were at last once more before the fire, shaking out our skirts. In the crackling quiet, music still welled up from the Winter Garden. Yet it was time to go. The whole business had taken a lot out of the Duchess. She was sadly bent. "I have done what I can. The rest is up to you." She stroked a tangled whisker.

But how?

"You are their mice. Your fates are intertwined with theirs."

"But—"

"I can only get your humans to the reception. I am myself never up at that hour. You must take charge. You cannot leave important decisions to humans. Times come when mice must pay their way. Your time draws nigh."

She dismissed us with a small nod. The firelight caught in her rusty tiara. We dropped three numb little curtsies, and turned to go.

And there stood . . . Lamont. Johnny-on-the-spot.

We supposed he had come for us, but he cleared his throat importantly and kept his tail well out of sight. "Lord Peter 'Enslowe!" he announced, stepping aside.

And there was the best-looking mouse you ever laid your eyes on, bowing past us to the Duchess.

The best-looking mouse you ever laid your eyes on.

Wonderfully trimmed whiskers. Very aristocratic ears. A tail that was pure poetry. I try to be sensible, but I was much moved. Louise's eyes bulged out of her head. Beatrice quivered. Who wouldn't?

"Ah, Lord Peter, how good of you to call," sang out the Duchess, rallying behind us. "Allow me to present the sisters Cranston. Helena."

I inclined my head in a genteel manner.

"Louise," said the Duchess.

Louise did the same.

"And Beatrice," the Duchess concluded.

Beatrice curtsied all the way to the carpet in a froth of flustered skirts. I thought we'd have to help her back up.

Lord Peter, Mouse-in-Waiting—no, that's not the term—Mouse Equerry to the human Lord Peter Henslowe, and even better looking.

But now Lamont was peering around this splendid titled mouse. "You three," he piped at us. "It's time you 'ightailed it for 'ome."

CHAPTER TEN

Camilla's Train

A S THE EVENING of the royal reception approached, the time drew nigh to pay our way. But how should we even *get* to the Royal Suite? We bickered for days—rough days and smooth, under Camilla's bed, and at our end of the yardstick.

"We will have to go on our humans," Louise said. "After all, they're on the guest list. We aren't. We can't just sashay up there and slip ourselves under the door. We might be seen or stepped on." How sure Louise was. How annoying.

On the afternoon their invitation arrived, the air was rent by the Upstairs Cranstons' screams, echoing along the corridor and far out to sea. Mostly from Mrs. Cranston.

"A Princess's reception? *A Royal Command?*" she shrieked, dithering. "Whatever shall I wear?"

"What indeed?" Louise remarked under Camilla's bed. "I shudder to think."

We all did.

"I shall have to infest Camilla and go to the reception on her," Louise decided.

"I don't mind going on Mrs. Cranston," Beatrice said, "as long as she doesn't wear her squirrels. I know my way around her."

And so, for once, *Beatrice* wasn't the problem. Evidently *I* was.

"Louise," I said, "I'll go with you on Camilla."

"Indeed you will not," she sniffed. "It will be hard enough to find a place for one of us to hide on her, let alone two. Besides, if Camilla should notice me somewhere on her person, she wouldn't be alarmed."

"Ha! Louise," I retorted, "she couldn't tell me from you at the lifeboat drill. 'Oh, Mousie!' she cried. She can't tell one mouse from—"

"She would certainly notice if there were two of us," Louise said. "She can count. Besides, Helena, Camilla is *my* human."

Oh, that was meant to sting, and it did. I bristled, *this close* to rage.

Then Louise said, "You can go on Olive." Very offhand.

I blew up. My head nearly hit the bedsprings. "You know perfectly well Olive won't be going. She's still flat on her back in her cabin with her head in a basin and the doctor calling three times a day. You know that, Louise. You have made this whole business about you and Camilla. You always do."

"But isn't *Olive* the whole business?" Beatrice butted in. We were nose to nose to nose.

"Isn't it all about giving Olive Her Chance and husband-hunting for her?"

"Be quiet," we said. But she had a point.

ON THE NIGHT of the royal reception as Olive moaned piteously in the next cabin, Camilla dressed for hours on end. At last she sent the maids away and examined herself in the mirror. And I must say, she looked nice.

Her dress may have been all wrong, but it was a pleasing pink, girlish like herself. Around the waist Camilla was only as big as a minute, in human terms. She was quite dainty, if I can say that about someone seven hundred times my size.

She dabbed toilet water behind her ears and plucked at her cheeks. Her sweet-sixteen pearls nestled in the hollow of her throat. On her shoulder was a corsage of two white orchids sent by her father from the ship's florist. Two white orchids tied up with ribbon. Hanging

down from the flowers, gray against pink, was
an inch or two of mouse tail.

Louise.

Camilla did not appear to notice that her corsage had a tail. She drew on her long white gloves,
fitted each finger, and reached for her evening bag.
It was a silver mesh reticule on a chain.

You are thinking that I was inside that evening bag. I tried. But no, I hadn't been able to
open the clasp. It was very tight.

Camilla turned to go. I had only this moment
and not another. She was just walking out
the door when I shot from under the bed and
hurled myself at the train of her dress. It was
only a short train and flouncy at the hem. I clung
to it as it dragged across carpet. It was the best
I could do. If she gathered up her train, I didn't
know where I'd be. I remembered Plunkett's
brim and clung on like death.

In the corridor she hurried to catch up with
her mother and father. Her train switched back

and forth, back and forth. I could only hope that Beatrice had infested Mrs. Cranston up ahead. I could see nothing but the pink silk of Camilla's train, which was right for my coloring.

Oh, just imagine bumping up those stairs— at sea—on the train of a dress that rippled from step to step. I was knocked six ways from Sunday. It was touch and go all the way to the very doors of the Royal Suite.

Fear like a fog rose from all three Upstairs Cranstons before those mighty doors. They were flanked by two big footmen in powdered wigs and braided coats, satin knee britches and white stockings. Buckle shoes. Guardians of the Royal Gate.

I could only glimpse them from the floor. They were enormous. The doors fell open. A human voice, English, blared and echoed:

MR. AND MRS. FLOYD CRANSTON
MISS CAMILLA CRANSTON

And into the Royal Presence we went, all six

of us, and all uncertain of our fates. But there was no time to dawdle.

The English voice was announcing the next guests behind us:

THE EARL AND COUNTESS OF CLOVELLY

Oh, how hard it is to make sense of a social occasion from the train of a dress. I dragged through a thicket of black trouser legs and satin knee britches and billowing skirts. In all this milling about somebody was apt to step on Camilla's train. I ducked and dodged till my head throbbed. I bobbed and wove for what seemed hours.

Camilla's moment seemed to come. She moved forward, wobbling. A shadow fell over me. Camilla was curtsying . . . to the Princess. She trembled all the way down her train.

You do not speak to royalty first. Royalty speaks first.

But a blatting voice butted in, and it was not royalty.

"My stars and garters, Princess, what grand quarters you have here. I'd hate to think what you're paying." The thundering voice went on, regardless. "If only my Olive could be present. We were hoping to give Olive Her Chance. But, poor girl, she's sicker than a poisoned pup. I don't know where it's all coming from!"

Mrs. Cranston.

Silence fell. You could hear the distant throb of the ship's engines. The fire crackled at the top of its lungs. We were doomed.

I chanced a wan peek out of the flounce. A figure in gunmetal gray skirts spoke in a hushed but blaring tone to the room in general.

"Who on earth is that extraordinary woman?" It was a very grand tone. Very scary. "That woman with the voice like the cawing of a crow and those shoulders like sides of beef?"

Oh no, Mrs. Cranston was showing her shoulders.

Camilla quaked. The voice went on. "She

cannot possibly be on the guest list. Now, where *is* that guest list?"

The gunmetal skirts whipped away. It had to be Lady Augusta Drear, Lady-in-Waiting to the Princess. Who else?

Camilla sagged. "Oh, Mama," she murmured so low that only I heard. Well, Louise and I.

Clearly, we were all to be rounded up and thrown out. Maybe even overboard. Camilla too. It wouldn't take Lady Augusta forever to nail her as a Cranston.

But in that moment another voice rang out, a royal one. "Let there be music!"

Relief rose in the room. Violins tuned. Chairs shuffled. Would they throw us out of the Royal Presence in the midst of a musical selection? I cowered in the train, one uncertain hand drawn up. Here again, I couldn't see a moment ahead. The room was settling. Gloved hands eased a gilt chair beneath Camilla.

In a quick and girlish gesture, she gathered

her skirts to sit. I grabbed for pink silk a second too late. She gave her train a quick twitch, and I flew out of it as from a slingshot. I arched through the air in the candlelit room, whiskers over teacup. The string quartet struck up Johann Strauss . . . *Die Fledermaus*.

I was in the air only a moment. But long enough to recall that I'd spent the whole of my life keeping my distance from humans. Now, every time I went near one, I was launched like a rocket. It was so unfair.

I was heading for the ancient Marquess of Tilbury, a large target. He lolled in his wheelchair. I landed on the claret-red velvet of his bulging evening coat. Just above the pocket handkerchief, a paisley foulard. It could have been worse. I could have cleared his slumping shoulder entirely and lit in the fire. Lit indeed. I dropped into the Marquess's pocket behind the handkerchief. My heart raced. I rose and fell with his labored breathing.

When I could pull myself together, I parted two points of the pocket handkerchief and beheld the sumptuous room.

My breath caught at its magnificence. Pale ladies on gilt chairs, their skirts arranged, the candle flame playing across their jewels. The gentlemen standing, studies in black and white with wing collars and kid gloves.

There just across from the Marquess and me sat Camilla. Her pretty face was pinched in fear. Her hands worked in her pink lap. I could just about read her mind. She was wondering if she should make a run for it before she was thrown out by a couple of big footmen.

As I watched, she glanced up. Standing very near to her was Lord Peter Henslowe. His gloved hands were clasped behind him above the tails of his coat. His wing collar flared below his chiseled chin. Lord Peter Henslowe, twenty-four and good-looking and hard to catch. He glanced down at Camilla, far down, bowing slightly. Camilla just inclined her head. The fire found the lights in her naturally wavy hair, fixed by a small jewel. She was too young to have her hair up. It flowed down her back.

The music played on while at the other end of the room, Lady Augusta Drear, tall as a crane, ransacked the Chippendale desk for the guest list. Before her on a cut-velvet divan sat ... Princess Louise, fourth daughter of the Queen of England.

I looked my first upon human royalty and beheld her grandeur. She was not a young woman, but handsome in a sharp-featured way. You wouldn't want to cross her or speak out of turn. She sat at her ease in cascading black net sprayed with diamonds. But her spine did not touch the back of the divan. No lady's should. No princess's does. Behind her, Lady Augusta shuffled all the papers on the desk to the strains of Johann Strauss.

It was warm in here: the crackling fire, the

blazing candles. The Marquess of Tilbury's doddering hand rose to his pocket handkerchief. He pulled it out of his breast pocket and me with it. He didn't notice that his pocket handkerchief had a tail. Then he mopped his perspiring brow with me. I was all over his forehead and the dome of his pate. It was disgusting. I was damp through. Then I was thrust back with the handkerchief into his pocket, nose and whiskers first. I liked to never get turned around.

When I could see out again, there at the far end of the room, Lady Augusta Drear held up a page of cream-laid paper in awful triumph. Had she detected a forgery even by candlelight? Was that evidence in her hand? The music began to wind down.

Time wasn't just running out; it was galloping like a mad horse. Camilla's gaze met Lord Peter Henslowe's. And in that very moment before Lord Peter looked away, Louise sprang up out of the orchid corsage and onto Camilla's shoulder. Light on her feet and quicker than thought, Louise darted around to the back of Camilla's neck. Camilla felt something, but her gaze was all tangled with Lord Peter's.

And then what do you suppose happened?

Just as the music stopped, Camilla's string of pearls broke. Pearls leaped from the hollow of her throat, bounced off her bodice, and peppered the floor. Pearls pattered along with the applause. Lord Peter Henslowe was on one knee before her, fishing for pearls at the hem of Camilla's pink skirts. "Oh," breathed Camilla, her hand on her throat, her feet crossed at the ankle. And Louise back in her orchids. Quick-thinking, sharp-toothed Louise. You have to hand it to her.

Lord Peter held up a kid-gloved palm full of pearls like an offering. Camilla blushed to match her dress. And like a galleon on stormy seas, Lady Augusta Drear barged down the room. She sailed past the violinists, scattering sheet

Quick-thinking, sharp-toothed Louise.

music. She was gunning for Mr. and Mrs. Cranston. Everyone seemed to look their way, showing the way.

They were marooned in the midst of the room. Purple-faced Mr. Cranston on his feet, half strangled by his collar, miserable in his spanking new tailcoat with the too-long sleeves. Below him sat Mrs. Cranston, overflowing a gilt chair. Her hair was dressed high above the great moon of her face. The cameo at her throat was the size of a stove lid. Her mountainous bare shoulders gleamed in the candlelight, and the top part of her ball gown struggled to contain her. She was a very generously built woman. A terrible shadow fell across her before she even noticed in her dithering way that something might be amiss.

In all innocence, she looked up at the awful visage of Lady Augusta. Not a handsome woman. The room held its breath. Fans froze. Again we heard the ship's engines throb.

Lady Augusta unclenched her mouth to speak. "Madam—"

But at that moment—that exact moment— Beatrice suddenly appeared out of Mrs. Cranston's ball gown. The front part, right in the middle, if you can picture it. There was hardly room, but Beatrice fought her way upward into open country. Her little pointed, bewhiskered face popped up like the cork out of a bottle. Two perky ears pointed north against Mrs. Cranston's bare flesh, below the cameo.

Saucy Beatrice looked up, beady-eyed, to catch Lady Augusta's attention. Lady Augusta was mortally afraid of mice, and there one was in the last place you'd think to look. Beatrice twitched her whiskers and batted her eyes.

The guest list dropped from Lady Augusta's hand and swooped to the carpet. Her eyes rolled back, and she fainted in slow motion, revolving as she went. Gunmetal corded silk crumpled. Quicker than he looked, Mr. Cranston scooped

Her little pointed, bewhiskered face popped up.

her up just before she landed. She hung, open-mouthed, in his big gloved hands, out cold.

He was the hero of the moment.

"I have an idea it's the heat," Mrs. Cranston told everyone. She dithered for her fan. "The poor old thing," meaning Lady Augusta. "Somebody ought to loosen her stays and cut her out of her corsets. I'm hotter than a firecracker myself, and wringing wet!"

Mrs. Cranston tapped herself with her fan, just where Beatrice had been. But Beatrice had made herself scarce.

THAT CONCLUDED the musical portion of the evening. A collation of light refreshments followed. Lord Peter Henslowe brought a small gold-banded plate of supper to Camilla where she sat demurely with her loose pearls in her purse and a corsage watchful on her shoulder.

CHAPTER ELEVEN

Sebastian's Secret Sweet Shop

T HE CANDLES GUTTERED, and the fire burned low. The party glittered to a close. The Princess rose, and all the room rose with her, except for the Marquess of Tilbury and me. His valet fed him one last spoonful of supper and dabbed his chins. Then we were rolling off down the passageway.

Beatrice and Louise could ride their humans home. I'd have to watch for the moment to spring out of the Marquess's breast pocket and find my own way.

Alas, I lingered too long.

Straight ahead of us at the end of the corridor was a thing called an elevator. It was a small, electrified room that moved up and down between decks. I never saw such a thing and wondered how it worked. And so I stayed on the Marquess too long. Curiosity killed the you-know-what.

A small male human in a bandbox hat and many buttons operated the elevator. There was barely room for us inside, as the Marquess was immense. We dropped from deck to deck. My stomach was up around my ears. Finally we were being pulled backward out on the Marquess's deck.

Then he sneezed.

A big wet one. I was ready to leap, but he reached for his pocket handkerchief, the paisley foulard, and seized on me instead.

He drew me out, leaving the handkerchief behind. I was in his great soft hand. A gold ring circled his smallest finger. One of my feet braced on that. He lifted me up, and we were nose to nose. He was one sagging wrinkle after another. But rank is more important than appearance.

His watery old eyes widened. His snowy eyebrows rose. Somehow he had me by the tip of the tail, holding me up. Never in my life had I been held up by the tail. Never. I was terrified, and embarrassed to death.

He dangled me. My hands scrabbled in thin air. My feet hung.

"Hee, hee," the Marquess said. "Hickory Dickory Dock!" He held me up for the valet to see. The wheelchair swerved.

"Oh, my lord, I should let it go," said the valet. "You don't know where it's been."

Then the Marquess sneezed again, or this story would have taken a different turn. The corridor was drafty. He reached for his handkerchief. I dropped through space. I bounced off his knee, turned once in the air, and lit running. I ran for my life, on all fours and tail high. Wherever I was, I needed to be somewhere else.

I ran down one passageway after another, up decks and down. I was like a . . . rat in a maze. I ran toward music, an orchestra playing a ragtime tune. I swerved another way and heard the sound of pool cue against ball. I ran where humans were, beneath their very feet. A lady switched her skirts aside. "Eeeek," she said. A walking stick swatted very near my throbbing tail. A polished shoe stamped. I bounded off of bulkheads. I raced through a fanning door, and skidded on open deck. I drew up by a coil of rope, very near the end of mine.

Damp wind cut my eyes. I huddled, shaking in my fur. There beyond the railing tossed the endless black and unforgiving sea. Water, water, everywhere. Above in the night the sparks from the funnels spiraled upward to join the firmament of stars. A terrible and lonesome beauty, and I was far from the tufted jewelry box of my bed.

I allowed myself a single whimper, but only one. The sea air whistled through my mind. My tail throbbed. My head rang. My hands wrung. Still, I pulled myself together, there in the shadow of the coiled rope.

In the next moment or the moment after that, I knew I wasn't alone. The sea made a swishing sound, but there was this other sound too. Nearer, much nearer.

My ears rose to perfect points. It was the sound of claws digging into rope, climbing. A nearly silent scraping, but there's nothing wrong with our hearing. I froze. Then above me a dark shadow loomed over the coiling rope, against the starry sky.

I dared look up at the awful outline of two ragged ears. Then—oh, the horror—a single burning eye, a sickening yellow. It was the ship's cat, one-eyed thanks to Nigel. And kill-crazy, as cats are.

I was numb, naturally, but alert. Another

Oh, the horror—a single burning eye, a sickening yellow.

scrabble as the ship's cat gathered his back paws for a sudden leap. I sensed his hindquarters swaying in anticipation, his tail coiling like the rope. He was fixing to pounce.

And there I was just below, with nothing between us but thin night air.

A horrid hiss arched above me from the airborne one-eyed cat. His claws would be stretched wide, his fangs winking by starlight.

I went blind and deaf for an instant. In my mind's eye flashed an awful scene from out of the past. I saw the corncob Papa had been working on when the barn cat pounced, all that time ago.

Then I was traveling as the ship's cat dropped with a thump upon the deck where I'd just been. The deck was slick, but I am quick.

I had to get back inside the ship. Otherwise I could be chased off this pitching deck and into the fathomless sea. The cat lost a moment, wondering where I went. A door fanned, and I made

for it, swerving. Trying to stay on the blind side
of a one-eyed cat is uphill work. I shot through
the door into the ship, hoping it would swing
shut in that feline face—slam him one, right on
the nose.

But luck was not with me. He was through
that door and on my tail. Now I ran at random.
My feet went faster than my thoughts. I might
have been headed anywhere, even onto the ballroom floor beneath the heedless feet of all those
milling humans.

Instead, I seemed to skim over the carpet of
a corridor. It was a deck nearly as grand as the
Princess's Royal Suite. Maids bustled from door
to door, carrying bed linens. I fled too fast to
be seen. But they couldn't miss the snarling cat.
With any luck, a maid would fetch him a good
swift kick in the other direction.

It wasn't to be. I picked the first closed door,
and was under it in a furry flash. Without a
second to spare. If cats could get under doors,

there'd be fewer mice. Far fewer. Hisses issued from the corridor side. Claws scratched at the doorsill. I seemed to feel hot cat breath even through the solid door. His chattering jaws rattled in my head. I sagged there, gathering myself.

The cabin before me was shrouded and dim. But darkness is nothing to a mouse. Another door was cut into one of the walls, so this must be part of a suite, possibly a grand one. Starlight showed through a porthole. Beneath it was a bed, a small one. I crept my way there and jumped up on it, with just enough spring left to lift me. Maybe I thought I'd be safer there, this far from the hissing door. I wasn't.

All manner of strange shapes littered the bed. Before I could make sense of them, light flooded. A hand had switched on the electrified lamp.

Somebody was in the bed. I liked to have fainted.

I froze of course, one hand drawn up, my eyes staring.

Two eyes stared back, small blue ones above enormous pink cheeks. It was that boy from the lifeboat drill. Lord . . . Sandown, the future Earl of Clovelly. Five years old and possibly a handful. He may have sensed me leaping onto the foot of his bed. I didn't have Louise's light way of bounding up on humans' beds. I didn't have the practice.

We stared at each other, up and down the rumpled blanket. It was littered with his toys. The rubber ball. A drum with sticks. A nutcracker in the shape of a foreign soldier. A cast-iron royal coach with four horses. Boys live in this kind of clutter. I was reminded of Lamont's bedroom. The collar buttons, the birds' bones, the ball of twine. The mess.

Another hiss came from beyond the door. I nearly lost hope then. I'd spent the whole of my life keeping my distance from cats and humans. Now look at me.

Little Lord Sandown peered down his bed,

blinking and interested. His round head was a mass of golden curls. He stuck a pudgy finger into one of his cheeks.

"I say," he said. "Are you real or a toy? Do you wind up? Where is your key?"

My key? Oh for heaven's sake. Still, I was the only living thing on this bed. Everything else was a toy. I couldn't think what to do. Then I rose up and turned slowly around, doing something graceful with my tail, until we were eye to eye again. And he could plainly see there was no key sticking out of my back. The idea.

I thought he might give me a good swat when he saw I was a true mouse. You know how humans are. But his finger was still in his cheek, and his other hand clutched the sheet. On his snowy nightshirt was a small crest, worked in gold thread. I awaited my fate. I was too tired to run. Too discouraged.

"Oh, you're real." He shot a sideways glance to one of the doors. Not the hissing door. The other one. "Would you like to play with my toys?" He was whispering, but of course it was past his bedtime.

I blinked at him. He had better manners than you'd expect, but how could I play with his toys? The ball was ten times my size. I could hardly lift one of those drumsticks. And the teeth on that soldier-shaped nutcracker were terrifying.

What would Louise do? She had the background for this sort of thing. I just shrugged my shoulders, though I don't really have any.

Little Lord Sandown thought and thought. You could nearly hear his brain turning over. I saw he was lonely. A lonely little human boy who needed company.

He leaned nearer and peered at me through the two blanketed mounds of his pudgy legs. "Are you hungry?" he muttered. "Could you eat a little something?"

Suddenly, I was starved. I certainly hadn't had

a bite to eat at the Princess's reception. I'd either been on somebody's train or in somebody's pocket or being hurled through the air. I was so hungry I could eat a horsefly.

I had never communicated with a human in my life. But now I nodded. It did not come naturally to me, but I saw how Louise did it.

"Well, then," said Little Lord Sandown, diving under his covers. "Sweets?" he said from under them. "Licorice all-sorts?"

His head reappeared. His golden curls were tousled now. He held up a somewhat furry morsel of blackest licorice. Which I've always hated.

I shook my head.

"No?" he said. "Well then. . . ." He popped it into his own mouth and vanished under the covers again. "Biscuit?" He reappeared with a pale cookie. "Scottish shortbread?"

That was more like it. I nodded prettily and tucked my chin, though I don't really have—

"There are chocolate creme sandwiches too

and a bit of fruitcake," His Lordship reported, "and most of a jam tart."

No wonder he was almost perfectly round. He slid the shortbread down the bed to me. In mouse terms it was the size of a bath mat. But as I say, I was starved. I tried to pick it up, but it was just that much too big.

Instead, I reared back, sat upright and made one hop, like a flea, onto the shortbread. It broke in half. Little Lord Sandown watched with interest as I picked up a shortbread half and began to nibble its edges. I have a dainty way of nibbling, and it was absolutely delicious. So buttery. His Lordship was fascinated. He nearly forgot to cram first one and then two chocolate creme sandwiches into his mouth.

I began to see how he thought. And in fact he was thinking about the jam tart. How at ease I was with a human! I wouldn't have dreamed it. I suppose it is best to start with their children, who have open minds.

But it was all too good to last. With a terrible suddenness, everything happened at once.

After only a quick clatter of keys, the door to the corridor flew open. A maid barged in, bearing a pile of fresh towels. I nearly jumped out of my fur. Two shortbread crumbs went down the wrong way. But worse was to come. Far worse.

From around the maid's aproned skirts there appeared a single cat's eye, a sickening yellow. That dastardly cat had lurked in the shadows by the door. Now his patience was rewarded. He lunged, upending the maid. Her feet went out from under her, and the air was full of unfolding towels. The cat was in the room, breathing hard and snarling. Patchy fur stood tall down his curving spine. The maid sprawled on her back, screaming.

The cat was making for the bed. I went the only place I could think to go.

Little Lord Sandown looked up with interest at the screaming, snarling room. He'd been licking the crumbs of a chocolate creme sandwich off his fingers when the one-eyed, kill-crazy cat made a run for the bed.

It was a nightmare. But by then I was inside the miniature cast-iron royal coach. It was a close fit, but I was entirely inside it except for my tail. I peered out like a furry gray Queen Victoria.

The ship's cat was in the air, then on the bed, digging in. His fangs dripped. He knew where I was, just past His Lordship's right foot, in my carriage, there behind the four cast-iron horses.

The ghastly cat's hackles grew higher as he meant to pounce and claw me out. But Lord Sandown merely took up the soldier-shaped nutcracker and brought it down squarely between the ragged ears. The cat keeled.

"Bad kitty," said His Lordship.

BUT THIS WAS only the beginning.

The other door flew open, and in strode Lord

"Bad kitty," said His Lordship.

Sandown's prune-faced nanny. She loomed into the room in a starchy nightdress, and her sparse hair was tied up in rags. In her grip was a hairbrush I didn't like the look of.

The maid was up in a crouch now, gathering the bath towels, making her quick escape and banging the door behind her.

"What is the meaning of this dreadful din?" barked the nanny in a fearful voice.

I had worked my way out of the royal coach from a window on the far side. Now I was under the blanket, but I could hear everything from here. The nanny clumped closer.

"Why is your light on, young Sebastian? Why are you not fast asleep, you wretched child?"

Only small sounds came from Lord Sandown—Sebastian. He was shrinking lower in the bed. I remembered the hairbrush and seemed to know she'd used it on him before. He whimpered.

"Not to mention the presence of a dead cat in your bed," said the nanny, very disapproving.

Dead? The cat? I was so encouraged by this news I peered out from under the blanket.

The nanny was just picking up the ship's cat by its tail. He had a ringed tail, absolutely hideous. She held him high with his forepaws dangling, like a lady's fur piece in terrible taste. But almost at once he hissed slightly, so he wasn't dead at all.

Holding him high, the nanny carried him to the door and pitched him into the corridor. He hit the far wall, snarled all the way down to the carpet, and shot away.

I only hoped he'd learned his lesson about chasing mice, or at least me. But you can't knock sense into a cat. People think cats are wise and have deep thoughts. They don't. But they do have nine lives, which is too bad.

As the nanny turned back to us, I slipped back under the blanket, and for good measure, the sheet. I crept along down there beside Sebastian's round body, and walked directly into a cupcake. It was disgusting. My whole head went in. I was plastered with icing and covered with crumbs. I stumbled backward, tripping on my tail, and sat suddenly on a chocolate-covered cherry. This bed was like a bakery shop and a candy store. And of course everything sticky. Including me, from stem to stern.

Now above me the nanny was discovering that Sebastian's teeth were coal-black from that licorice.

"EATING?" she boomed. "After you've BRUSHED YOUR TEETH? Stuffing your awful pudding face when you ought to be FAST ASLEEP?"

Oh she was fierce, and so *rude*.

In two seconds she'd be stripping the bed. She'd be looking for Sebastian's secret supply of treats, and guess who she'd find?

Besides, she was itching to use that hairbrush on His Lordship's backside. She hadn't brought it along to brush his tousled curls.

As I tried to plan my next move, the nanny made hers. She dragged Lord Sebastian out of the bed by one of his ears. And this pulled both blanket and sheet halfway off the bed and me.

There I stood just where the blanket stopped, completely iced in pink frosting. Just like the cupcake beside me. You couldn't tell us apart. And of course the caved-in chocolate-covered cherry, at least half a dozen Scottish shortbreads, a generous slice of fruitcake, and that jam tart. There was everything in this bed but a three-layer cake with candles.

Lord Sandown hung from the nanny's grip by an ear, whimpering. Her mean eyes widened. This quick glimpse of Sebastian's secret sweet shop was all she needed. I don't think she saw me. I was pink all over and could easily pass as a pastry.

"No, please, Nanny Pratt!" Sebastian cried.

The raised hairbrush threw a shadow on the wall. "Please, not the hairbrush!"

My heart was in my mouth. But then the door

to the corridor opened. There stood a lady. A tall and stately human. Diamonds wound round and round her swan-like neck. Her evening gown was shimmering midnight blue, draped.

This lady saw the shadow of the hairbrush upon the wall and gasped. Her eyes snapped.

"Mummy!" shrieked little Lord Sebastian, twisting in Nanny Pratt's gnarled hand.

Mummy. So this would be the Countess of Clovelly. I went to work at once.

"Nanny Pratt!" Sebastian's mother said. "What is the meaning of this?"

The hairbrush fell to the floor. Sebastian followed. Nanny Pratt had turned him loose, a moment too late. Her hands, now free, worked before her. I suppose they did. I was too busy to notice.

"Come to Mummy," cried the Countess of Clovelly. She dropped to one shimmering knee, and Little Lord Sandown raced into her arms. They clung.

Then the Countess of Clovelly said to Nanny Pratt, "How dare you raise a hand—a *weapon*—to this defenseless child! Explain yourself at once, woman."

Woman!

Nanny Pratt gibbered.

"I am waiting," said the Countess in quite a worrying voice.

"I acted only for his own good, my lady, in my usual way," Nanny Pratt said in a wobbly voice. "He stuffs himself with unwholesome treats that he hides in his bed. He is sly, my lady, and greedy and must be corrected. And all the foodstuffs in his bed are apt to attract vermin. Vermin, my lady."

Vermin indeed.

The Countess rose slowly. She took clinging Sebastian by the hand.

"Show me these unwholesome treats he hides in his bed, Nanny Pratt," she said grandly. She wasn't a countess for nothing. She advanced upon the bed, and Nanny Pratt stood aside to show her the evidence.

The Countess looked far down her perfect nose upon the rumpled bed. Sebastian looked too. "I see a great many things in this bed," the Countess remarked. "A drum with sticks. A coach and four. An India rubber ball, and a nutcracker. Nothing remotely edible."

"But, my lady." Nanny Pratt looked again at the bed. There wasn't a crumb on it. Not a Scottish shortbread or jam tart or fruitcake slice. The cupcake was missing, along with the chocolate-covered cherry. I had stuffed them all down the space between the bed and the wall in two of the busiest minutes of my life. I was at that moment enjoying a much-needed rest, under the top sheet.

After a moment of heavy silence, the Countess of Clovelly spoke. "Pratt, you may withdraw. And once this ship has docked, your services will no longer be required."

"But, my lady—"

"Pack your traps, Pratt," said Her Ladyship, "and be gone."

I SLIPPED AWAY later, after I'd rubbed the worst of the pink frosting out of my fur. Honestly, I stuck to everything. Then once things had finally settled down and the light was out and little Lord Sebastian was asleep, I stole away. He slept very peacefully without that hairbrush hanging over his head. He had thrown one pudgy hand back upon his pillow. In his other was the nutcracker soldier.

I had taken a long way home indeed from the Princess's reception and the Marquess's pocket. But it had not been a bad night's work. A wicked nanny had been dispatched, thanks to my quick thinking and even quicker work. I believe in giving credit where credit is due, and I was due some.

Moreover, from this night forth, Louise wasn't

the only one with a human. And *mine* had been born with a title.

I worked myself under Lord Sandown's door and into the night. I was absolutely exhausted, and longed for my jewelry case. But I was far from there, and this endless night held yet another surprise to shock me half out of my fur. Read on.

Secrets the Dark Night Keeps

WE TAKE PRIDE in finding our way home, we mice. But I dragged from deck to deck, half asleep on my feet. Still, I kept one eye out for the cat who might be keeping one eye out for me.

At long last I was on the right deck. I slumped through the carpet, weaving along the creaking, sleeping ship. A little woozy, I slipped beneath a cabin door. But cautious. Always cautious.

Surely my sisters were home before me. A

shaded light burned within. Camilla was not in the bed. Nor Louise at the foot of it. I looked underneath. No eyes glowed from there. Beatrice was making herself scarce.

But the cabin was not empty. Far from it. A young lady sat on the dressing-table bench, turned away to the only chair. She wore something gauzy, softly draped: a gown for receiving a guest. Her hand extended to a gentleman there in the chair. Immaculate black and white. Wing collar. A good head of hair, center-parted.

He was a stranger to me. But I knew who he was, who he had to be. *Well, I'll be a monkey's uncle*, I thought to myself as my eyes liked to pop out of my head. He leaned forward over the young lady's hand. He kissed it.

Oh dear. Humans kissing. I went beet-red under my frosted-pink fur. I didn't know where to look, and I was all eyes. My hand drew up uncertainly in that way I have.

"My darling," the doctor said.

I nearly passed out. Now I was scrambling back, wiggling under the door, once more in flight.

I hadn't been in Camilla's cabin at all.

I'd been in Olive's.

And I'd just witnessed Olive being kissed by the doctor.

Oh, what secrets the dark night keeps.

I darted on down to the next door and squirmed under it, dizzy with what I'd witnessed. Home at last. But where was my breath? It took forever to find.

And there was Camilla, in her flannel nightie, climbing into her bed. Louise was just bounding up on the foot of it. I had not been missed. Camilla was eager to tell Louise all about the evening, every detail. And Louise was eager to pretend she didn't already know. Her little head cocked, all ears.

Neither of them could be bothered to notice me soaring up on the dressing table, dropping into the tufted jewelry case, beside the orchid corsage. No one was eager to hear of *my* adventures, which were every bit as exciting as anybody else's. Every bit.

Though at one point Camilla said, "Why am I smelling cake?"

And that would be me.

At least there was more room in the jewelry case now that Camilla's pearls were gone and would have to be restrung. I was unstrung myself. My head and tail tingled. Beatrice was already there, sound asleep. Her nose found my ear. "Oh stop at once," she murmured, deep in some unsuitable dream. "I implore you."

ON THE DAYS that followed, the entire ship could talk of nothing but the sudden romance that had broken out between Camilla and Lord Peter Henslowe. A whirlwind romance had burst into being at a royal reception with the breaking of a string of pearls. But that's the way with an ocean voyage: Dynasties have been decided.

Camilla hardly had time to change her clothes five times a day. For breakfast, then a turn on the deck with Lord Peter. For lunch and then their game of shuffleboard. For tea and yet again for dinner. She was in and out of the cabin, and so were her maids. We three, Louise and Beatrice and I, bickered under the bed for days.

"Thanks to *me*," Louise endlessly recalled, "Camilla has snagged Lord Peter Henslowe, a major catch. Truly top-notch. His family—the Henslowes, you know—have two castles and a house in London. They ride to hounds. *Hounds*, my dears. Lord Peter will be an earl one day, and that will make Camilla a countess. A *countess*." Oh how Louise preened. She grinned and grinned to show her useful teeth. We were meant to remember pearls pattering at a certain social occasion.

"A countess is, of course, a useful thing to be," I observed. "I am myself slightly acquainted with the Countess of Clovelly."

Louise bristled. "The Countess of Clovelly?

Don't be absurd, Helena. You don't know any humans."

But then Beatrice, who never listens, butted in. "Isn't Camilla too young—"

"Not for a lord," know-it-all Louise replied. "And his is an ancient family."

I cleared my throat. "We are ourselves a very old fam—"

"Well, if it hadn't been for *me*," said Beatrice, horning in again, "all the Upstairs Cranstons would have been thrown bodily out of the Princess's reception, and us with them. I snatched them from certain social shame. I saved all our bacon. Fortunately, I know my way around Mrs. Cranston."

Beatrice popped her eyes and waggled her whiskers as she'd done from the top of Mrs. Cranston's ball gown.

Oh how they preened, my proud sisters. I merely sat back, my tail arranged, my hands gathered before me. I had a secret or two up my furry sleeve that would send them staggering, if I chose to share it. If and when. I—Helena, the oldest.

"You are looking very smug, Helena," Louise remarked. "I can't think why."

LAMONT FOUND US bickering beneath the bed. A maid had just breezed out the door with Camilla's ironing. Lamont breezed in. "'Ello, 'ello," said the bothersome boy. "I cahn't linger, as I 'ave me duties. But 'ere's a delivery. Look wot it is!"

He'd pushed in among us. Now he sat back on his spindly shanks. In his hand was a bouquet: baby's breath and a stalk or two of lily of the valley, tastefully tied up in thread. Hothouse blooms, no doubt from the florist's floor.

"Compliments of 'Is Lordship, Peter Henslowe, Mouse Equerry to the 'uman one. Me and 'im is good mates now. Me and the Mouse Equerry."

"The Mouse Equerry and I," I said.

"The Mouse Equerry and I," said Lamont.

How well we recalled Lord Peter's bow, past

us to the Duchess. Those aristocratic ears. The tail that was pure poetry. Rank *and* appearance, and plenty of both.

We were lost in thought. The ship rose on a swell, hung there, then settled, then rose again. Though no moan came from Olive's cabin.

Louise found her voice. "Who are those flowers for?"

Sly Lamont made us wait, spinning out the moment. Then he handed the bouquet over to Beatrice.

"Me?" She pointed an innocent finger at herself. "How nice."

"It *would* be Beatrice," Louise muttered. "How typical of the entire male sex. Honestly. They go for her type every time."

Beatrice stuck her nose in the flowers. A stalk of lily of the valley curled around one of her ears.

Louise's brain was running riot. She babbled on. "Still, since Camilla is going to end up as Her Ladyship, married to Lord Peter Henslowe and living in two castles and their London place, I will naturally make my home with them. Camilla and I have never been parted, you know. We'll be quite English. And I assume there'll be servants."

Louise nodded rather grandly to Beatrice, who was sniffing her flowers. "Beatrice and the mouse—Lord Peter will of course play a role in our establishment."

Beatrice sniffed her flowers. Louise preened. How suddenly she'd sketched out an entire future for Beatrice and herself. I was left out, and I was hurt. But would I let that show? You know better than that.

"Do not put your cart before your horse, Louise," I merely said, rearranging my hands. "There's many a slip betwixt cup and lip. Rome wasn't built in a day."

"Rome?" Beatrice looked up from her bouquet. "Are we going to Rome? Where is it?"

❧　❧　❧　❧　❧

WE WERE ALMOST in sight of land now. Beams from European lighthouses swept the nighttime horizon. Too excited to sleep, Camilla chattered till all hours to listening Louise.

I tossed and turned. Then when I slept, I dreamed a familiar dream. In it Beatrice sat silently up. She rose and picked her way across the hatpins. Then she was gone like a puff of smoke.

I awoke with a start and saw it was true. I was alone in the night and the jewelry case, with nothing beside me but a crushed stalk of lily of the valley.

Beatrice was gone.

I lay there, bolt awake. Then a face appeared above the lock, peering in. It was Louise. "Move over," she whispered. "Camilla is using her chamber pot."

There was certainly enough room. "Where's Beatrice?" Louise asked, settling.

"You tell me," I whispered back.

"Honestly, that girl," Louise said. "She will throw away the chance of a lifetime and lose her reputation. You should have kept an eye on her, Helena."

"Yes, I suppose I should have," I sniffed, "since I have nothing else to do and no life of my own." I sniffed again for good measure.

"On the other hand," I observed, "Beatrice may be up on the open deck with Mouse Equerry Lord Peter this very minute. A rendezvous. They may be whispering sweet nothings into each other's ears, and planning a future."

"We can only hope," Louise sighed. "Beatrice does seem to have him on the hook. Now if she can only reel him in. Honestly, they go for her type every time."

With that Louise went sound asleep on the crushed lily of the valley. I tossed until dawn broke through the portholes. Then back Beatrice came. She was just about to drop into the jewelry case when she saw Louise's sleeping form. She drew up a hand. Then she nuzzled in between us. Her nose nestled near my ear, and she snored convincingly.

But I was not deceived.

CHAPTER THIRTEEN

Dynasty and Destiny

THROUGH THE MIRACLE of the wireless telegraph, news of the whirlwind romance between Camilla Cranston and Lord Peter Henslowe reached two continents before we docked. Evidently the London newspapers were full of it, and the New York papers took note. There are no secrets at sea.

With every account, Lord Peter's family grew more ancient, their castles bigger. And Camilla grew richer and richer: an American heiress. The Heiress of the Year. It was a story that had everything because Lord Peter was thought to be hard to catch. And Camilla had caught him just by being herself.

"A pearl at any price," the newspapers called her. They scrambled for photographs of her. When they couldn't find any, they ran pictures of other girls entirely, and called them Camilla.

We were the talk of the ship, even Louise and Beatrice and I. Being, as we were, Cranstons ourselves. And Camilla was not our only claim to fame. No indeed. A rumor had swept the ship of a secret engagement between the Mouse Equerry Lord Peter and . . . Miss Beatrice Cranston, of all mice. I don't know how that rumor started. Certainly not with me. I blamed Louise.

We were the talk of the ship. At dinner Cecil led us to the best yardstick, and mice stood on their spools for a better look at us. The room glowed with eyes upon us. Mice we had not met wanted to know us now. New York City mice.

There were mice of the Vanderbilt family on this crossing, and even they glanced our way. We basked. Beatrice wore a sprig of baby's breath over one ear. Fame is a funny thing. Fame is like a secret. Both are hard to keep.

BUT IT WAS our last night at sea before word reached Mr. Cranston. He was often the last to know anything. I believe he picked up the news about Camilla and Lord Peter Henslowe in the gentlemen's billiard room, or someplace where men gossip.

The biggest steamer trunk stood open on the floor of Camilla's cabin. The room was a beehive. Maids rushed about, raising dust, folding Camilla's clothes, dressing her for dinner. Probably fussing with her hair.

We three, Louise and Beatrice and I, couldn't see everything from under the bed. The steamer trunk blocked the view. Flowers for Camilla from Lord Peter crammed the cabin, sprays and baskets of them. There wasn't room to swing a you-know-what.

The dinner gong sounded through the ship, and the door banged open. It was Mr. Cranston, no doubt filling it up. We saw only the big knobs of his shoes.

"OUT!" he howled, scattering the maids. We jumped and huddled. He strode in.

Behind him hovered Mrs. Cranston. She was back in her ball gown. We recognized the skirts—changeable watered taffeta.

"Now, Floyd," she said, dithering. "Now, Floyd."

"What's this I hear about you and some English . . . twerp?" he thundered at Camilla.

Twerp? We quaked, under the bed.

Camilla was there at her dressing table. I believe she might have been pulling on her gloves, fitting them over each finger. "He is Lord Peter Henslowe, Papa," she said, strangely calm and sure of herself.

"I don't care if he's the King of England!"

roared Mr. Cranston, putting his big foot down.

"There is no King of England, Papa," Camilla said. "There's a queen. Queen Victoria."

"AND I DON'T CARE ABOUT HER EITHER," Mr. Cranston bellowed. You could have heard him throughout this British ship.

"I hope this Lord Peter What's-His-Name doesn't think you're rich!"

"No, Papa," Camilla replied. "I have told him we are poor. Poor as church mice."

We goggled at one another, under the bed.

"POOR!" Mr. Cranston boomed. "Girl, if we were poor, you wouldn't be traveling first class!"

"Now, Floyd," Mrs. Cranston said.

Mr. Cranston turned on Mrs. Cranston. "I blame all this on you, Flora," he barked. "I lay all this at your door. We have not blundered off to the ends of the earth to marry *this* girl off. She's only sixteen years old!"

"Seventeen, Papa," said Camilla, cool as anything. "Eighteen in the fall. I will have my hair up by then. Peter and I will gladly wait six months. After all, it will take that much time to plan the wedding."

"Oh! The wedding!" Mrs. Cranston cried. "The wedding! What shall I wear?"

An awful silence fell. Fumes seemed to rise from Mr. Cranston. Sulfurous fumes. "Six months?" he said in a low and dangerous voice. "Six *months?*" Once again he rounded on Mrs. Cranston. "Woman," he said, "you seem to forget this whole business was to get Olive off our—to get Olive married. NOT CAMILLA!"

"Now, Floyd—"

"It will take Olive more than six months. It's liable to take Olive SIX YEARS!"

"No, it won't, Papa."

Though there was hardly room, someone new had entered Camilla's cabin. Someone in a long, gauzy gown, pea-green.

It was Olive.

All the other Upstairs Cranstons turned to

her. Louise and Beatrice and I crept nearly out into the light, drawn by this scene. We gazed all the way up Olive. On her best days, she was sallow, but this evening she wasn't as pea-green as her dress. She looked quite dignified in an older-sister way. She looked nice.

"I am myself engaged to be married, Papa."

Mr. Cranston liked to have bulged out of his wing collar. "What the—"

"To the ship's doctor, Papa. Dr. Fanshawe."

You could have heard a pin drop. Mr. Cranston's mouth moved and moved before any sound came out. "I suppose this Dr. What's-His-Name is another English twerp!"

"No, Papa. He's from Cleveland."

Mr. Cranston's face was an alarming shade of deep purple now. "Well, I hope he doesn't think we're rich!"

"Oh yes, Papa. I told him you were the richest man in Westchester County," Olive replied. "But he said he would marry me anyway."

Olive smiled. Quite a pleasant smile. "You see, I haven't been sick since the lifeboat drill. I've just been seeing the doctor."

Another astonished silence fell. In fact, it came crashing down. Far below us the ship's engines throbbed.

Mrs. Cranston reeled, then rallied. "A doctor? My Olive's marrying a *doctor!*"

The heavens seemed to open. Mrs. Cranston threw her arms around Olive, then reached for Camilla. They danced in all the space there was. They did jigs and fandangos. They kicked in their skirts, a dance of joy and triumph. Mr. Cranston was caught somewhere in the middle.

We drew back under Camilla's bed to keep from being trampled and mashed flat. The noise was deafening. "Two weddings!" Mrs. Cranston shrieked. "Two weddings!"

Beatrice and Louise were struck almost dumb with surprise.

"Olive, of all humans, finding a husband

A dance of joy and triumph.

entirely on her own!" Louise goggled. "Is that not the most surprising thing you ever heard in your entire life, Helena?"

"Actually, it is not." I gathered my hands. "I've known about it for some while."

"Helena, you couldn't have," Louise said, and Beatrice agreed. "Olive has spent the whole voyage in her cabin, where you have never been."

"As it happens, I *was* in her cabin, possibly at the very moment of their betrothal. There was some kissing."

"Then why didn't you tell?"

"I wasn't asked." I sniffed, slightly.

WHEN THE UPSTAIRS Cranstons were finally gone, Lamont squeezed himself in under the door.

"'Ere, you three," he said in his awful accent. "You'll be late for your dinner. It's Gala Night in the mouse dining saloon. There'll be confetti, flaming pudding, and three cheeses: a boursin

au poivre, a pecorino Romano, and an Emmen-
thaler—that's the one with the 'oles. Dancing to
follow."

We stirred.

"I will meself conduct you," he said grandly.
"I know all the shortcuts now. Get you there in
'arf the time. I know this ship like the back of
me 'and."

"Hand, Lamont," I said.

"'And," he said.

"Then we can all four have dinner together,"
I said. "It will be like our first night. Like old
times." I gathered us all up, in my mind.

Lamont sat back on his shanks and pointed
at himself. "Me? I don't 'ave dinner with passengers. I'm *crew*."

"Lamont, we are not passengers. We're family."

"Card-carrying crew," he said. "I 'ave me
papers. I've signed on and shipped out."

"Lamont, you don't mean—"

"I'll be pursuing a career as Assistant Cabin

Steward, with prospects." He drew himself up, as much as he could. "It's me destiny."

Destiny. Where did he even learn the word?

We gazed at our brother, trying to think. You know how mice are about water. And Lamont meant to spend his life at sea. You can't make these things up.

"Oh, Lamont." I worked my hands. The bothersome boy! "What if something happens to your tail? Who will sew it back?"

But he thrust his patchy tail well out of sight and turned his little pointy, chinless face to the future.

CHAPTER FOURTEEN

Waltz Time

CURLS OF TICKER tape in the national colors coiled along the yardsticks of our gala dinner. Confetti fell on our fur. We made an entrance, Louise and Beatrice and I, and we were noticed. Vanderbilts noticed.

But then Cecil's voice rang out: "Be upstanding for Her Royal Highness, the Duchess of Cheddar Gorge!"

Spools skidded back, and the room rose. There was the Duchess, though she rarely partook in public. She was a bit more bent than before, on her gold-topped matchstick. But then she was nearing home. Cecil slid the bone china chair beneath her. As I came out of my curtsy, the Duchess waved me into the place beside her, only a whisker away. I had Beatrice on my other side, where I could keep an eye on her. Then Louise, all eyes. We were, of course, at the best yardstick.

The Duchess glanced down at the soup with disdain. It was a brown Windsor. "We believe," she said just over our heads, "that we can congratulate ourselves on a notably successful voyage."

Louise leaned around us to say, "Dynasties have been decided!"

"Quite," said the Duchess. "It has been brought to our attention that your Cranstons are dining with both their future sons-in-law at the captain's table. *The captain's table* on the last night at sea! A triumph! And there is a rumor of champagne."

We inclined our heads with modest pride. You do what you can.

"How well events have worked out." The Duchess's rusty tiara twinkled. Her old lips pursed, over the terrible teeth.

"And we have seen the last of that nasty Nanny Pratt," I remarked. "She was lucky indeed that the Countess of Clovelly did not drop her overboard. She is lucky that she is not food for the fishes at this very moment."

This news did not seem to hold the Duchess's attention. But Louise blinked. "Who in the world is Nanny Pratt?" she said.

"She is the former nanny of little Lord Sandown," I replied. "She has been sent packing."

"And how would you possibly know all that, Helena?" Louise goggled. Even Beatrice paid attention.

"Because Lord Sebastian Sandown is *my* human, Louise." And so he had been, for a very important evening of his young life.

And that was the end of that because a waiter stepped between us, with a serving of beef Wellington crumbs.

The waiters swooped and scraped. Vegetables were being served, though the English boil all their vegetables to death.

But the Duchess only picked at her food. She fetched up a sigh.

"Poor Lady Augusta Drear, Lady-in-Waiting to the Princess, has not had a happy crossing," she said, waggling her old head. "She is high-strung and has not been herself since that fainting fit she had on the evening of the reception."

Beatrice was all ears. She wiggled them.

"They will be taking her down the gangplank on a stretcher tomorrow, trussed up like a parcel." The Duchess pulled a long face. "It is thought that Lady Augusta will have to go away for a cure." Again the Duchess sighed. "This will only add to our many duties. We are, as you will imagine, very active behind the scene."

Her gaze grazed me. "You cannot think how busy we are in the Queen's Diamond Jubilee year. Sixty years upon the greatest throne in human history! Royals will flock to the Palace from abroad and naturally bring their mice. Germans—the Liederkranzes and the Limburgs. And the Havartis from Denmark. A real infestation. Meals! Beds! And everyone so touchy about where they are seated at table."

The Duchess's mind made lists before our very eyes. Her thoughts seemed to tangle like her whiskers. She shook her old head and looked quite pitiful. But it seemed to me she stole a stealthy look in my direction. A sly look. I felt the royal glance. Her old hand found mine. Just a small tap. "I wonder, my dear, if I can persuade you to come to my assistance?"

Me? Helena? How?

"I shall be in great need of another pair of hands as capable as yours. After all, my leaping days are behind me, and my climbing days are numbered. And now, without Lady Augusta Drear, my duties will be doubled."

The Duchess seemed to shrink up and look quite frail and needy.

I hung on her every word. So did Beatrice and Louise.

"I wonder, my dear, if you would consent to become an Assistant Mouse-in-Waiting for the Royal Princess Louise, daughter of the Queen. At the palace, of course. Buckingham Palace."

THE MURMURING, CHEEPING dining saloon seemed to fall away. Suddenly before my mind's eye rose the greatest palace on earth.

"Her Royal Highness occupies a suite at the very front of the palace with excellent views over London. I can promise you quarters within her very walls. And naturally a full staff."

My head went round in perfect circles. Louise and Beatrice were speechless.

"Only think, my dear," said the Duchess. "The

Diamond Jubilee and the Queen riding out in the royal landau under a black lace parasol. And with her daughters: the Princess Helena, the Princess Louise, the Princess Beatrice! How the flags will snap! How the bands will play! How the crowds will cheer as all the world watches!"

Crowds cheered in my head. I saw it all in my mind, just as I was meant to. I saw the gates of a royal palace swing open upon a future of my own.

"Take all the time you need to make your decision, my dear," said the Duchess, murmuring now. "A minute. Two minutes. Whatever you need."

MY MOUTH OPENED, then closed. Suddenly the room around us seemed to erupt. I'd forgotten that dancing was to follow the gala dinner. Spools shuffled. Even now the waiters were carrying away our yardsticks to make space for a ballroom floor. Tails were being rearranged throughout the dining saloon. The Duchess's china chair was positioned at the edge of the ballroom. Waiters lowered her into it. I handed her her matchstick.

But where was the music to come from? Musical instruments small enough for mouse hands and lips would hardly serve. Their sound would be reedy and tinny.

But we were in the great world now. It seemed the entire chorus of *The Nutcracker* would hum a selection of Viennese waltzes and quadrilles and gallops.

Then, only a few bars into "The Blue Danube" waltz, there among us strode Lord Peter, Mouse Equerry.

The room caught its breath. Oh, those wonderfully trimmed whiskers, those peerless ears. That tail of pure poetry. And just a whiff of bay rum aftershave lotion.

Murmurs rippled the room. Lord Peter never dined in public. But here he was now, scanning across us with aristocratic interest. His gaze fell upon the Duchess of Cheddar Gorge. She was already tapping her matchstick in waltz time.

Then Lord Peter was before her, with a neat bow from the neck as her hand came up. He took it and bowed deeper to kiss the air above it. Oh, the elegance of that moment. How many generations had it taken to produce mice-of-title such as these?

The Duchess gestured in our direction. Lord Peter favored both Louise and me with courtly nods. I suppose we simpered, but he only had eyes for Beatrice. I nudged her. The provoking girl was picking one last flake of confetti off her front fur.

Lord Peter bowed before her. His hand came out. Louise gave her a nudge that nearly sent her sprawling. Then—somehow—Beatrice and Lord Peter were on the ballroom floor. Only the two of them while the whole mouse world watched.

Panic gripped me as he took her in his arms.

Then—somehow—Beatrice and Lord Peter were on the ballroom floor.

Could the silly girl dance? We didn't. We never
had. When would we?

But as Lord Peter took one step forward, Beatrice took one step back. Her tail lashed prettily,
and they were swept away upon the blue Danube.
He of course never put a foot wrong as they
scampered in a perfect pattern, round and round
the floor. Oh, it was lovely. I wish you could have
seen them. Beatrice lolled in Lord Peter's arms,
keeping him at a little distance. There was something dreamy and faraway in her eyes. They were
far from beady. They were simply far away.

"Honestly," Louise murmured, "they go for
her type every time." But you had to admire Beatrice. She did not gloat, though Lord Peter was
on the hook, and our whole world knew it now.
There are no secrets at sea.

THEY DANCED AND danced until the ballroom
filled up with other couples. Tails are a problem
on a crowded ballroom floor, of course. But how

nimble and deft everyone was, taking their cue from Lord Peter and Beatrice. The old Duchess kept time with her matchstick.

Louise and I looked on. Louise sat with ankles crossed and hands folded together as much like Camilla as she could manage. But finally she could stand it no longer. Her nose was in my ear and she was whispering moistly.

"What are you going to tell the Duchess, Helena? Are you going to be an Assistant Mouse-in-Waiting or not? Are you going to live in the palace? The Duchess wants to know. I'm sure your two minutes are up by now," whispered Louise, though we mice are not good with time.

I merely nodded, having come to a decision. And when the Duchess turned to me, her missing eyebrows high, I was ready. As ready as I'd ever be.

"As to my future employment, Your Royal Highness," I said—very proper, very correct. "I will make you a deal."

The Duchess stared. "A deal?" Her matchstick

clattered to the floor. "A *deal?*" She looked nearly at me. "Is that some sort of *American* expression?"

"Yes, Duchess," I said. "It is."

For I had looked into the future by then. We were far from Aunt Fannie Fenimore's crystal ball. But I always look ahead anyhow. Somebody has to.

I scanned the future and saw—deep within a great gray and gold-tipped palace—a wondrous scene. There were sprays of white lily of the valley, artfully arranged, and petals of orange blossom.

I saw Beatrice there in the center of this scene, Beatrice blushing in white. And myself and Louise, tastefully attired and holding small nosegays of seasonal flowers. Bridesmaids.

And now I heard quite different music—a wedding march.

"Here's the deal, Duchess," I said. "I shall be honored to accept a position in your royal household if my sister can be married in a palace wedding."

The Duchess was thunderstruck. "A palace wedding?" She gripped her front fur. Her tiara quivered. "A *palace wedding* for a bride far from royal?"

I nodded and gathered my hands. Louise liked to pass out.

The Duchess pondered, and her old eyes narrowed. "Ah well," she breathed at last. And her breath nearly knocked both Louise and me off our spools. "I suppose something of the sort can be arranged." While behind her, Beatrice and Lord Peter turned and turned in one waltz after another.

And wedding bells rang in my mind.

CHAPTER FIFTEEN

A Fond Toodle-oo

JUST AT DAWN, tugboats nudged the great iron ship into the dock. Whistles blew, announcing our arrival. Beside Camilla's sleeping form her biggest steamer trunk yawned open. The men would be here for it very shortly. Outside, roustabouts were already . . . rousting about. Sea birds cawed. Somewhere beyond our portholes the gangplank rumbled down. Lady Augusta Drear was no doubt being carried ashore, trussed up like a parcel. Nanny Pratt was doubtless not far behind her, being packed off permanently.

Three small figures, gray as the dawn, gathered on the carpet of Camilla's cabin, nose to nose to nose. You know who. We were nearly tuckered out from the gala dinner with dancing to follow. It had gone on far into the night.

Now we had only moments to scale the trunk, up to Camilla's handkerchief drawer, for the journey on to London. The time had come once more to pack ourselves for shipping.

Louise was all aflutter the way she gets. Her tail flailed. "I wonder if I should wake Camilla? Scamper lightly across her face or something. If she oversleeps—"

"Up into the handkerchief drawer, Louise," I said. I have to see to everything.

"You first, Beatrice." I pointed up to the drawer. "Up you go."

And would you believe it? The provoking girl didn't budge. She stood stock-still, rooted to the rug. "*Me?*" she said, hand on furry front. "Helena, *I'm* not going to London, England, for pity's sake, wherever it is. The idea! I am only seeing you off. I am only here to bid you a fond toodle-oo." Her eyes popped and goggled. Her whiskers twitched. You never saw such astonishment.

Louise and I stared.

But Beatrice stared right back. "I thought it was perfectly clear," she said maddeningly. "I'm staying on the ship."

We liked to have turned to stone, Louise and I. The ship? Beatrice was staying on the ship? My heart sank. Where to begin with her? "Beatrice, first of all, you are terrified of water. And far more importantly, you are to be married in a palace wedding that I have personally arranged. A *palace wedding*, Beatrice, with—"

"Nigel and I have reached an understanding," she said, interrupting.

She looked modestly aside. Also, she would not meet my eye.

Nigel!

Those great white haunches. Those piercing ruby eyes. The commanding tail. Gorgeous whiskers. "'Ello, 'ello" indeed.

My eyes narrowed. "Beatrice, how did you manage that?"

She sat back and arranged her tail. "It was just the other night when I slipped away from the jewelry case. You know, the tufted one with the hatpins and—"

"Get on with it, Beatrice."

"And I told Nigel of Lord Peter's . . . interest in me. I mentioned the flowers. The baby's breath. The lily of the valley."

Ah. Once Nigel had a rival, it brought him around.

Nigel!

"But, Beatrice, you have just waltzed the night away in Lord Peter's arms. Lord Peter *Mouse Equerry*, Beatrice."

She turned up her hands in a very annoying way. "Oh, that was easy. There was nothing to it," she said. "I just pretended he was Nigel."

Louise moaned.

"Beatrice," I said reasonably, "you do understand Lord Peter's position in English society as Mouse Equerry, don't you? You grasp that one day it is entirely possible that you could be a mouse countess. A *countess*, Beatrice."

"Two castles," Louise said.

Beatrice goggled at us. "But I love Nigel. And naturally Nigel loves me," she said. "It was love at first sight."

With Beatrice it always is.

Outside the porthole, carts clattered. Voices called and cried. My head pounded. Time was running out. Time always is. Above us, Camilla was beginning to stir. Bedsprings creaked.

"Beatrice," I said to my provoking sister, "I will make you a deal."

Beatrice blinked.

CHAPTER SIXTEEN

A Palace Wedding

Q UEEN VICTORIA'S DIAMOND Jubilee
took place on a June day without a cloud
in the sky. "Queen's weather," as we call such days
here in England.

The gilded gates of Buckingham Palace fell
open that morning to the stately parade of the
Queen and all her mighty court.

The gentlemen, booted and spurred, on
stamping steeds. The little old Queen shaped
exactly like a teapot, with white feathers in her
bonnet. And with her in the open landau, Prin-

cess Helena—the human Helena, and quite a generously built woman. They were off across London to St. Paul's Cathedral to give thanks for the Queen's sixty years upon the greatest throne in human history.

Behind them in landaus of their own, drawn by white horses, came the other royal princesses. All of them nodding, nodding, to left and to right at the crowds cheering down the Mall. Oh that red and gold morning beneath the blue dome of sky, while all the world watched!

We liked to never get Her Royal Highness Princess Louise ready and downstairs into her carriage. None of her maids were any more use than Mrs. Flint's daughters back home. Lady Augusta Drear was naturally no longer in attendance. And the Princess's new lady-in-waiting, Lady Clementine Cumberbatch, didn't know where anything was. The Princess's royal suite was a perfect puzzle to her.

With everything in a muddle, the Duchess of

Cheddar Gorge and I were rushed off our feet. Then at the last moment, the heel came off of one of the Princess's shoes. I had to fling myself against the button to ring for the boot boy. And the Duchess had to show me which button. Honestly, without mice, where would humans be? Their heads are in the clouds.

An Assistant Mouse-in-Waiting's work is never done. The Duchess and I were two tired mice by the time the Princess rolled out of the palace gates, behind her royal mother, into the sea of flag-waving humans. We watched from a window looking out upon the Mall, the Duchess and I. And our day had barely begun.

All the hundreds of palace staff were watching now, clustered at their windows: the Pages of the Presence and the Pages of the Backstairs. The Body Linen Laundresses and the Bedchamber Women. The Fire Lighters and Footmen, the Butlers and Under Butlers. The Chimney Sweeps. The Apothecary to the Household.

Even the Rat Killer. Yes, there's an official palace Rat Killer. So useful.

A silence fell upon the palace then. No footsteps rang. No one was summoned or sent for. The palace awaited the Queen's return. Sunlight—pale, watery English sunlight—fell, almost unseen, across Princess Louise's personal drawing room. Sunbeams winked on the polished fender before the hearth. How welcome is a crackling fire on an English summer day.

Oh, you should have seen that noble chamber in all its quiet grandeur. The famous paintings on the paneled walls. The gently tinkling chandeliers. The tapestry cushions, personally worked by Princess Louise, who is artistic. Then, just at the stroke of noon, probably, there came a stirring and the occasional cheep.

The Persian carpet suddenly filled up with a murmuring multitude of mice. Out of the woodwork we came. You know how we are. Always just a whisker away, whether you know it or not.

But never so many in one place. All the palace mice, of course, and we greatly outnumber the humans. Greatly. And the mice of the better London families. Then the foreign mice visiting with their royal humans. The King of the Belgians alone was accompanied by a retinue of forty mice, and he was but one king among many. And yes, New York City mice. Vanderbilts. A major infestation. The carpet was gray with us.

There is nothing like a palace wedding to draw a fashionable crowd. And the flowers on the fender were much admired. Sprays and cascades of orange-bloom petals and lily of the valley, plucked straight from the palace greenhouse. The Duchess and I had been up half the night.

She went first, of course, the Duchess did, to her place at the front, to represent the mother of the bride. Down the aisle between the crowds she hobbled on her matchstick, wearing her rusty tiara and a caterpillar boa.

For music, the entire chorus of *The Nut-cracker* began to hum the wedding march. But they were rather drowned out by a military band, blaring now from the forecourt below the windows. And so Beatrice started down the aisle to the strains of "Rule, Britannia." She carried a burgeoning bouquet of four late violets, white ones, picked dew-fresh that very morning from a shady corner of the palace gardens.

The wedding guests made a path for her across the Persian carpet, leading to the fender before the hearth. She was a lovely bride, of course, and you know how Beatrice likes to be the center of attention. Several of the foreign mice dropped curtsies as she passed, not quite knowing whether she was royal or not.

From a small explosion of tulle between her ears, a train of point lace fully six inches long flowed down behind her. It was white lace, ivory with age—a snippet off Queen Victoria's own train from her long-ago wedding day.

At Beatrice's throat, hung from a length of dental floss, was a single pearl—one from Camilla's necklace that had escaped being restrung. Her wedding gown, ivory like her veil, was simple and girlish, and hiked at the rear to accommodate her tail. She has a pretty way of flailing it. And seven petticoats beneath, so she seemed to skim just above the pile of the carpet, like a floating doily. I ran up her dress myself, with the help of six or eight needle-mice of the palace staff.

Beatrice proceeded on the arm of Lamont, who had shore leave for the occasion. He sported a very tight wing collar and a small black bow tie that looked suspiciously like Cecil's. Being the man of the family, Lamont was to give Beatrice away. He was very much on his dignity. And he knew I was coming down the aisle right behind his unsightly tail.

I was naturally maid of honor. My bouquet was of three waxy begonias, pink to match my

She seemed to skim just above the carpet, like a floating doily.

dress, which is right for my coloring. Behind me came Louise as bridesmaid, completing our party. We are of course neighbors now, Louise and I, as the Henslowe family's London house is nearby the palace, only a whisker away. Louise was in lavender, which is more Camilla's color than hers. But we looked nice.

It was a day beyond our wildest dreams, and my eyes grew misty as we approached the fender. Then there before us was the clergy-mouse, come directly from Westminster Abbey. He wore a purple silk stole, embroidered, around his neck and held the tiniest prayer book you ever saw. And spectacles, which put me in mind of Aunt Fannie Fenimore from our old life.

Beside him stood the groom. Ramrod straight upon his mighty haunches. Snowy white fur. Ruby eyes. Gorgeous whiskers. Nigel.

Yes, Nigel. Also on shore leave for the occasion. I couldn't talk her out of him. It had been love at first sight, but I had insisted on a palace wedding. I'd put my foot down. You do what you can.

Lamont was leading Beatrice up to Nigel now. I busied myself arranging her veil and her tail. As she handed me her violets, she goggled her eyes at me and wiggled her ears. You know Beatrice. Then she turned to Nigel, and her future.

The clergy-mouse adjusted his spectacles to begin: "Dearly beloved . . ."

And my mind spun backward to our old lives, on the far side of all the surging sea. A moment flashed before me like a glimpse from deep within a crystal ball. There was the ancient humped figure of Aunt Fannie Fenimore. Bald patches, spectacles, and all: Aunt Fannie upon her powder puff throne.

I remembered the day I'd gone to her through the hedge to learn about our futures. I recalled her extending both her old hands stretched wide. "This is how you hold on to your family," she had said.

You hold them with open hands so they are free to find futures of their own. It's just that simple.

Before you knew it, Beatrice and Nigel were united in the bonds of matrimony, sealed with a kiss. And back up the aisle they proceeded. "'Ello, 'ello," said Nigel, nodding to left and to right as Beatrice hung on his arm. From below the windows in the forecourt, the military band struck up "God Save the Queen."

CAKE CRUMBS AND dancing followed. But the Duchess's dancing days were behind her. Palace servants seated her at the edge of the dance floor on a small silver ring box that belonged to Princess Louise. There she sat tapping time to the music with her matchstick.

The members of *The Nutcracker* chorus hummed "The Blue Danube" waltz, and Nigel and Beatrice took to the floor. It wasn't a proper ballroom floor. It was Persian carpet. But Nigel took Beatrice in his arms and stepped forward. She stepped back, and off they floated as all the mouse multitude pattered applause.

Then what do you suppose happened?

Out of nowhere appeared Lord Peter, Mouse Equerry. Only a whiff of bay rum aftershave, and there he was, bowing from the neck before the Duchess of Cheddar Gorge. Oh, those aristocratic ears! I never cease to marvel. If I am remembering correctly, he wore a silk cravat overflowing a grosgrain waistcoat from his London tailor. And a cutaway coat with tails. Two tails plus his own.

The Duchess's withered hand came up, and he kissed the air above it. She smiled up at him, showing her terrible teeth. Then she nodded in my direction.

And he was before me.

My heart skipped a beat. I buried my nose in my waxy begonias in a sudden fit of shyness. Under my fur I went pink as my dress.

But he waited until our eyes met. Then he spoke. "I hope you have saved this waltz for me, Miss Cranston. And many more besides."

Then I was in his arms. Don't ask me how. I don't dance. I never had. When would I? But we were turning and turning in the waltz, swept away upon the beautiful blue Danube, while all the world watched and wondered.

You should have seen the look on Louise's face.

Look for another adventure with
Richard Peck's

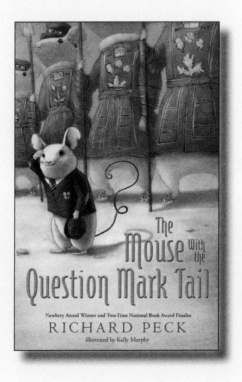

A companion to

Keep reading for a peek at
Richard Peck's Newbery Honor winning

A Long Way from Chicago

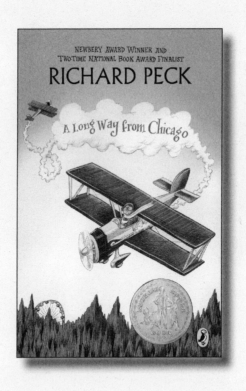

Prologue

———

It was always August when we spent a week with our grandma. I was Joey then, not Joe: Joey Dowdel, and my sister was Mary Alice. In our first visits we were still just kids, so we could hardly see her town because of Grandma. She was so big, and the town was so small. She was old too, or so we thought—old as the hills. And tough? She was tough as an old boot, or so we thought. As the years went by, though, Mary Alice and I grew up, and though Grandma never changed, we'd seem to see a different woman every summer.

Now I'm older than Grandma was then, quite a bit older. But as the time gets past me, I seem to remember more and more about those hot summer days and nights, and the last house in town, where Grandma lived. And Grandma. Are all my memories true? Every word, and growing truer with the years.

Shotgun Cheatham's Last Night Above Ground

———— ❦ ————

1929

You wouldn't think we'd have to leave Chicago to see a dead body. We were growing up there back in the bad old days of Al Capone and Bugs Moran. Just the winter before, they'd had the St. Valentine's Day Massacre over on North Clark Street. The city had such an evil reputation that the Thompson submachine gun was better known as a "Chicago typewriter."

But I'd grown to the age of nine, and my sister Mary Alice was seven, and we'd yet to see a stiff. We guessed that most of them were where you couldn't see them, at the bottom of Lake Michigan, wearing concrete overshoes.

No, we had to travel all the way down to our Grandma Dowdel's before we ever set eyes on a corpse. Dad said Mary Alice and I were getting to the age when we could travel on our own. He said it was time we spent a week with Grandma, who was getting on in years. We hadn't seen anything of her since we were tykes. Being Chicago people, Mother and Dad didn't have a car. And Grandma wasn't on the telephone.

"They're dumping us on her is what they're doing," Mary Alice said darkly. She suspected that Mother and Dad would take off for a week of fishing up in Wisconsin in our absence.

I didn't mind going because we went on the train, the Wabash Railroad's crack Blue Bird that left Dearborn Station every morning, bound for St. Louis. Grandma lived somewhere in between, in one of those towns the railroad tracks cut in two. People stood out on their porches to see the train go through.

Mary Alice said she couldn't stand the place. For one thing, at Grandma's you had to go outside to the privy. It stood just across from the cobhouse, a tumbledown shed full of stuff left there in Grandpa Dowdel's time. A big old snaggletoothed tomcat lived in the cobhouse, and as quick as you'd come out of the privy, he'd jump at you. Mary Alice hated that.

Mary Alice said there was nothing to do and nobody to do it with, so she'd tag after me, though I was two years older and a boy. We'd stroll uptown in those first days. It was only a short block of brick buildings: the bank, the insurance agency, Moore's Store, and The Coffee Pot Cafe, where the old saloon had stood. Prohibition was on in those days, which meant that selling liquor was against the law. So people made their own beer at home. They still had the tin roofs out over the sidewalk, and hitching rails. Most farmers came to town horse-drawn, though there were Fords, and the banker, L. J. Weidenbach, drove a Hupmobile.

It looked like a slow place to us. But that was before they buried Shotgun Cheatham. He might have made it unnoticed all the way to the grave except for his name. The county seat newspaper didn't want to run an obituary on anybody called Shotgun, but nobody knew any other name for him. This sparked attention from some of the bigger newspapers. One sent in a stringer to nose around The Coffee Pot Cafe for a human-interest story since it was August, a slow month for news.

The Coffee Pot was where people went to loaf, talk tall, and swap gossip. Mary Alice and I were of some interest when we dropped by because we were kin of Mrs. Dowdel's, who never set foot in the place. She said she liked to keep herself to herself, which was uphill work in a town like that.

Mary Alice and I carried the tale home that a suspicious type had come off the train in citified clothes and a stiff straw hat. He stuck out a mile and was asking around about Shotgun Cheatham. And he was taking notes.

Grandma had already heard it on the grapevine that Shotgun was no more, though she wasn't the first person people ran to with news. She wasn't what you'd call a popular woman. Grandpa Dowdel had been well thought of, but he was long gone.

That was the day she was working tomatoes on the

black iron range, and her kitchen was hot enough to steam the calendars off the wall. Her sleeves were turned back on her big arms. When she heard the town was apt to fill up with newspaper reporters, her jaw clenched.

Presently she said, "I'll tell you what that reporter's after. He wants to get the horselaugh on us because he thinks we're nothing but a bunch of hayseeds and no-'count country people. We are, but what business is it of his?"

"Who was Shotgun Cheatham anyway?" Mary Alice asked.

"He was just an old reprobate who lived poor and died broke," Grandma said. "Nobody went near him because he smelled like a polecat. He lived in a chicken coop, and now they'll have to burn it down."

To change the subject she said to me, "Here, you stir these tomatoes, and don't let them stick. I've stood in this heat till I'm half-cooked myself."

I didn't like kitchen work. Yesterday she'd done apple butter, and that hadn't been too bad. She made that outdoors over an open fire, and she'd put pennies in the caldron to keep it from sticking.

"Down at The Coffee Pot they say Shotgun rode with the James boys."

"Which James boys?" Grandma asked.

"Jesse James," I said, "and Frank."

"They wouldn't have had him," she said. "Anyhow, them Jameses was Missouri people."

"They were telling the reporter Shotgun killed a man and went to the penitentiary."

"Several around here done that," Grandma said, "though

I don't recall him being out of town any length of time. Who's doing all this talking?"

"A real old, humped-over lady with buck teeth," Mary Alice said.

"Cross-eyed?" Grandma said. "That'd be Effie Wilcox. You think she's ugly now, you should have seen her as a girl. And she'd talk you to death. Her tongue's attached in the middle and flaps at both ends." Grandma was over by the screen door for a breath of air.

"They said he'd notched his gun in six places," I said, pushing my luck. "They said the notches were either for banks he'd robbed or for sheriffs he'd shot."

"Was that Effie again? Never trust an ugly woman. She's got a grudge against the world," said Grandma, who was no oil painting herself. She fetched up a sigh. "I'll tell you how Shotgun got his name. He wasn't but about ten years old, and he wanted to go out and shoot quail with a bunch of older boys. He couldn't hit a barn wall from the inside, and he had a sty in one eye. They were out there in a pasture without a quail in sight, but Shotgun got all excited being with the big boys. He squeezed off a round and killed a cow. Down she went. If he'd been aiming at her, she'd have died of old age eventually. The boys took the gun off him, not knowing who he'd plug next. That's how he got the name, and it stuck to him like fly-paper. Any girl in town could have outshot him, and that includes me." Grandma jerked a thumb at herself.

She kept a twelve-gauge double-barreled Winchester Model 21 behind the woodbox, but we figured it had been Grandpa Dowdel's for shooting ducks. "And I wasn't no Annie Oakley myself, except with squirrels." Grandma was still at the door, fanning her apron. Then in the same voice she said, "Looks like we got company. Take them tomatoes off the fire."

A stranger was on the porch, and when Mary Alice and I crowded up behind Grandma to see, it was the reporter. He was sharp-faced, and he'd sweated through his hatband.

"What's your business?" Grandma said through screen wire, which was as friendly as she got.

"Ma'am, I'm making inquiries about the late Shotgun Cheatham." He shuffled his feet, wanting to get one of them in the door. Then he mopped up under his hat brim with a silk handkerchief. His Masonic ring had diamond chips in it.

"Who sent you to me?"

"I'm going door-to-door, ma'am. You know how you ladies love to talk. Bless your hearts, you'd all talk the hind leg off a mule."

Mary Alice and I both stared at that. We figured Grandma might grab up her broom to swat him off the porch. We'd already seen how she could make short work of peddlers even when they weren't lippy. And tramps didn't seem to mark her fence post. We suspected that you didn't get inside her house even if she knew you. But to our surprise she swept open the screen door and stepped out onto the porch. I followed. So did Mary Alice, once she was sure the snaggletoothed tom wasn't lurking around out there, waiting to pounce.

"You a newspaper reporter?" she said. "Peoria?" It was

the flashy clothes, but he looked surprised. "What they been telling you?"

"Looks like I got a good story by the tail," he said. " 'Last of the Old Owlhoot Gunslingers Goes to a Pauper's Grave.' That kind of angle. Ma'am, I wonder if you could help me flesh out the story some."

"Well, I got flesh to spare," Grandma said mildly. "Who's been talking to you?"

"It was mainly an elderly lady—"

"Ugly as sin, calls herself Wilcox?" Grandma said. "She's been in the state hospital for the insane until just here lately, but as a reporter I guess you nosed that out."

Mary Alice nudged me hard, and the reporter's eyes widened.

"They tell you how Shotgun come by his name?"

"Opinions seem to vary, ma'am."

"Ah well, fame is fleeting," Grandma said. "He got it in the Civil War."

The reporter's hand hovered over his breast pocket, where a notepad stuck out.

"Oh yes, Shotgun went right through the war with the Illinois Volunteers. Shiloh in the spring of sixty-two, and he was with U. S. Grant when Vicksburg fell. That's where he got his name. Grant give it to him, in fact. Shotgun didn't hold with government-issue firearms. He shot rebels with his old Remington pump-action that he'd used to kill quail back here at home."

Now Mary Alice was yanking on my shirttail. We knew kids lie all the time, but Grandma was no kid, and she could tell some whoppers. Of course the reporter had been lied to big-time up at the cafe, but Grandma's lies were more interesting, even historical. They made Shotgun look better while they left Effie Wilcox in the dust.

"He was always a crack shot," she said, winding down. "Come home from the war with a line of medals bigger than his chest."

"And yet he died penniless," the reporter said in a thoughtful voice.

"Oh well, he'd sold off them medals and give the money to war widows and orphans."

A change crossed the reporter's narrow face. Shotgun had gone from kill-crazy gunslinger to war-hero marksman. Philanthropist, even. He fumbled his notepad out and was scribbling. He thought he'd hit pay dirt with Grandma. "It's all a matter of record," she said. "You could look it up."

He was ready to wire in a new story: "Civil War Hero Handpicked by U. S. Grant Called to the Great Campground in the Sky." Something like that. "And he never married?"

"Never did," Grandma said. "He broke Effie Wilcox's heart. She's bitter still, as you see."

"And now he goes to a pauper's grave with none to mark his passing," the reporter said, which may have been a sample of his writing style.

"They tell you that?" Grandma said. "They're pulling your leg, sonny. You drop by The Coffee Pot and tell them you heard that Shotgun's being buried from my house with full honors. He'll spend his last night above ground in my front room, and you're invited."

The reporter backed down the porch stairs, staggering under all this new material. "Much obliged, ma'am," he said.

"Happy to help," Grandma said.

Mary Alice had turned loose of my shirttail. What little we knew about grown-ups didn't seem to cover Grandma. She turned on us. "Now I've got to change my shoes and walk all the way up to the lumberyard in this heat," she said, as if she hadn't brought it all on herself. Up at the lumberyard they'd be knocking together Shotgun Cheatham's coffin and sending the bill to the county, and Grandma had to tell them to bring that coffin to her house, with Shotgun in it.

By nightfall a green pine coffin stood on two sawhorses in the bay window of the front room, and people milled in the yard. They couldn't see Shotgun from there because the coffin lid blocked the view. Besides, a heavy gauze hung from the open lid and down over the front of the coffin to veil him. Shotgun hadn't been exactly fresh when they'd discovered his body. Grandma had flung open every window, but there was a peculiar smell in the room. I'd only had one look at him when they'd carried in the coffin, and that was enough. I'll tell you just two things about him. He didn't have his teeth in, and he was wearing bib overalls.

The people in the yard still couldn't believe Grandma was holding open house. This didn't stop the reporter who was haunting the parlor, looking for more flesh to add to his story. And it didn't stop Mrs. L. J. Weidenbach, the banker's wife, who came leading her father, an ancient codger half her size in full Civil War Union blue.

"We are here to pay our respects at this sad time," Mrs. Weidenbach said when Grandma let them in. "When I told Daddy that Shotgun had been decorated by U. S. Grant and wounded three times at Bull Run, it brought it all back to him, and we had to come." Her old daddy wore a forage cap and a decoration from the Grand Army of the Republic, and he seemed to have no idea where he was. She led him up to the coffin, where they admired the flowers. Grandma had planted a pitcher of glads from her garden at either end of the pine box. In each pitcher she'd stuck an American flag.

A few more people willing to brave Grandma came and went, but finally we were down to the reporter, who'd settled into the best chair, still nosing for news. Then who appeared at the front door but Mrs. Effie Wilcox, in a hat.

"Mrs. Dowdel, I've come to set with you overnight and see our brave old soldier through his Last Watch."

In those days people sat up with a corpse through the final night before burial. I'd have bet money Grandma wouldn't let Mrs. Wilcox in for a quick look, let alone overnight. But of course Grandma was putting on the best show possible to pull wool over the reporter's eyes. Little though she seemed to think of townspeople, she thought less of strangers. Grandma waved Mrs. Wilcox inside, and in she came, her eyes all over the place. She made for the coffin, stared at the blank white gauze, and said, "Don't he look natural?"

Then she drew up a chair next to the reporter. He flinched because he had it on good authority that she'd just been let out of an insane asylum. "Warm, ain't it?" she said straight at him, but looking everywhere.

The crowd outside finally dispersed. Mary Alice and I hung at the edge of the room, too curious to be anywhere else.

"If you're here for the long haul," Grandma said to the reporter, "how about a beer?" He looked encouraged, and Grandma left him to Mrs. Wilcox, which was meant as a punishment. She came back with three of her home brews, cellar-cool. She brewed beer to drink herself, but these three bottles were to see the reporter through the night. She wouldn't have expected her worst enemy, Effie Wilcox, to drink alcohol in front of a man.

In normal circumstances the family recalls stories about the departed to pass the long night hours. But these circumstances weren't normal, and quite a bit had already been recalled about Shotgun Cheatham anyway.

Only a single lamp burned, and as midnight drew on, the glads drooped in their pitchers. I was wedged in a corner, beginning to doze, and Mary Alice was sound asleep on a throw rug. After the second beer the reporter lolled, visions of Shotgun's Civil War glories no doubt dancing in his head. You could hear the tick of the kitchen clock. Grandma's chin would drop, then jerk back. Mrs. Wilcox had been humming "Rock of Ages," but tapered off after "let me hide myself in thee."

Then there was the quietest sound you ever heard. Somewhere between a rustle and a whisper. It brought me around, and I saw Grandma sit forward and cock her head. I blinked to make sure I was awake, and the whole world seemed to listen. Not a leaf trembled outside.

But the gauze that hung down over the open coffin moved. Twitched.

Except for Mary Alice, we all saw it. The reporter sat bolt upright, and Mrs. Wilcox made a little sound.

Then nothing.

Then the gauze rippled as if a hand had passed across it from the other side, and in one place it wrinkled into a wad as if somebody had snagged it. As if a feeble hand had reached up from the coffin depths in one last desperate attempt to live before the dirt was shoveled in.

Every hair on my head stood up.

"Naw," Mrs. Wilcox said, strangling. She pulled back in her chair, and her hat went forward. "Naw!"

The reporter had his chair arms in a death grip. "Sweet mother of—"

But Grandma rocketed out of her chair. "Whoa, Shotgun!" she bellowed. "You've had your time, boy. You don't get no more!"

She galloped out of the room faster than I could believe. The reporter was riveted, and Mrs. Wilcox was sinking fast.

Quicker than it takes to tell, Grandma was back, and already raised to her aproned shoulder was the twelve-gauge Winchester from behind the woodbox. She swung it wildly around the room, skimming Mrs. Wilcox's hat, and took aim at the gauze that draped the yawning coffin. Then she squeezed off a round.

I thought that sound would bring the house down around us. I couldn't hear right for a week. Grandma roared out, "Rest in peace, you old—" Then she let fly with the other barrel.

The reporter came out of the chair and whipped completely around in a circle. Beer bottles went everywhere. The straight route to the front door was in Grandma's line of fire, and he didn't have the presence of mind to realize she'd already discharged both barrels. He went out a side window, headfirst, leaving his hat and his notepad behind. Which he feared more, the living dead or Grandma's aim, he didn't tarry to tell. Mrs. Wilcox was on her feet, hollering, "The dead is walking, and Mrs. Dowdel's gunning for me!" She cut and ran out the door and into the night.

When the screen door snapped to behind her, silence fell. Mary Alice hadn't moved. The first explosion had blasted her awake, but she naturally thought that Grandma had killed her, so she didn't bother to budge. She says the whole experience gave her nightmares for years after.

A burned-powder haze hung in the room, cutting the smell of Shotgun Cheatham. The white gauze was black rags now, and Grandma had blown the lid clear of the coffin. She'd have blown out all three windows in the bay, except they were open. As it was, she'd pitted her woodwork bad and topped the snowball bushes outside. But apart from scattered shot, she hadn't disfigured Shotgun Cheatham any more than he already was.

Grandma stood there savoring the silence. Then she turned toward the kitchen with the twelve-gauge loose in her hand. "Time you kids was in bed," she said as she trudged past us.

Apart from Grandma herself, I was the only one who'd seen her big old snaggletoothed tomcat streak out of the coffin and over the windowsill when she let fire. And I supposed she'd seen him climb in, which gave her ideas. It was the cat, sitting smug on Shotgun Cheatham's breathless chest, who'd batted at the gauze the way a cat will. And he sure lit out the way he'd come when Grandma fired just over his ragged ears, as he'd probably used up eight lives already.

The cat in the coffin gave Grandma Dowdel her chance. She didn't seem to have any time for Effie Wilcox, whose tongue flapped at both ends, but she had even less for newspaper reporters who think your business is theirs. Courtesy of the cat, she'd fired a round, so to speak, in the direction of each.

Though she didn't gloat, she looked satisfied. It certainly fleshed out her reputation and gave people new reason to leave her in peace. The story of Shotgun Cheatham's last night above ground kept The Coffee Pot Cafe fully engaged for the rest of our visit that summer. It was a story that grew in the telling in one of those little towns where there's always time to ponder all the different kinds of truth.